VULGARIAN RHAPSODY

VULGARIAN RHAPSODY

A NOVEL

ALVIN ORLOFF

THREE ROOMS PRESS
New York, NY

Vulgarian Rhapsody
A NOVEL BY Alvin Orloff

ISBN 978-1-953103-38-3 (trade paperback)
ISBN 978-1-953103-39-0 (Epub)
Library of Congress Control Number: 2023934212

TRP-106

Publication Date: October 17, 2023

BISAC Coding:
FIC011000 Fiction / LGBTQ+ / Gay
FIC014000 Fiction / Historical
FIC064000 Fiction / Absurdist
FIC082000 Fiction / Own Voices

ACKNOWLEDGEMENTS:
Chapter 9: "Dougie Doodles and The Enchanted Gay Bar" was originally published
(in slightly altered format) in *Instant City: A Literary Exploration of San Francisco*
Issue No. 8, Spring 2013

Chapter 22, "Boiler Room" was orignally published (in slightly altered format)
in *Eleven Eleven Journal*, Issue 12, Winter 2012

COVER AND BOOK DESIGN:
KG Design International: www.katgeorges.com

DISTRIBUTED IN THE U.S. AND INTERNATIONALLY BY:
Publishers Group West: www.pgw.com

Three Rooms Press | New York, NY
www.threeroomspress.com | info@threeroomspress.com

Dedicated with love, reverence,
and a bit of exasperation to
Princess Pretty Pie and Cap'n Cuddles

VULGARIAN RHAPSODY

CHAPTER 1

INTRODUCING HARRIS

You've probably seen Harris around town. He possesses a remarkable talent for just sort of *turning up*. Go to a magazine rack and there he'll be, leafing through an Italian *Vogue* with a studied, almost theatrical air of nonchalance. Visit Macy's and you'll find him leisurely sniffing colognes with the judgmental scowl of a wine connoisseur. Drop by a Walgreens and, sure enough, there he is again, rolling his eyes at the skin rejuvenators as if expressing dissatisfaction for some invisible audience. You're apt to discover him lurking in the corner of dive bars, hanging out in the kitchen at house parties, and perusing the gourmet cheese at the supermarket. Harris is actually rather hard to avoid.

Very well, you say (impatiently sneaking a glance at the clock on your cell phone) perhaps I have crossed paths with this Harris chap. What exactly does he look like? In answer, he's somewhere between twenty-five and fifty-two, but one would be hard pressed to say where because his face displays a timelessly haggard quality. He's of

European peasant stock, short, and with the low center of gravity necessary for harvesting potatoes and baling hay. His complexion is both wan and ruddy, his hair limp and sandy brown. He has an unremarkable nose, a tedious mustache, and thin, unkissable lips. The only clue that Harris is a person worthy of interest is found in his eyes, which are entirely too lively and malicious for his drab, ordinary face.

As for his wardrobe, Harris favors two distinct styles. The first is the retro "white-trash" look perennially popular with gay hipsters who want to bask in irony but still sort of butch it up. Think trucker hats with odd slogans, plaid shirts, and vintage denim. Alternately, he attempts a "metrosexual" look involving things like relaxed suit jackets and white pants. He is not someone you or anyone would long to see in the latest sandals, but he will always have the latest sandals. Shoes are one of Harris's few luxuries.

That surprises you? Ah, I see. The fancy retail establishments he haunts have you imagining an affluent member of the shopping classes.

Allow me to clarify: Harris reads imported fashion magazines at newsstands because he cannot afford to purchase them. He does not buy cologne at department stores, but instead anoints himself daily from the free tester bottles. And he was rolling his eyes not at the selection, but the prices of the moisturizers. Harris (much like I, your humble narrator) is a gentleman living in what were once, in a more tactful age, referred to as "reduced circumstances."

Despite his haughty airs, Harris is no social climber. Rather he is in the grip of that once typically homosexual passion for cultivated taste. He is an aesthete, but no snob, just as capable of rhapsodizing over pot and garage rock as white wine and opera. Wealth and class are incidental to Harris's idea of glamour. He worships only *chic*. Harris terms those without *chic* "vulgarians" and does his best to avoid them. This is, alas, impossible since, by his reckoning, such persons constitute well over ninety percent of the population.

A telling fact: Harris regards his name as a serious affliction, an impediment to better living. He would prefer to be called Desmond, Adrian, or Jacques: something sophisticated and perhaps a little French. Harris is a name, he believes, appropriate only for the roadies of Scottish heavy metal bands or alcoholic horse trainers. Why doesn't Harris change his name? The reason is simple: Harris changes nothing. Even if there were a store where names were sold in charming little boxes tied up with ribbons, a store with sleekly attractive salesclerks and a generous exchange policy, he *still* wouldn't buy or purchase one. He could never afford it.

What if the names were reasonably priced? you ask. What if the store accepted all major credit cards or sold on the installment plan with no money down? The answer is still no. Harris is congenitally unable to marshal his resources to purchase anything of quality other than fancy footwear and alcohol. No doubt scientists are staring at double helixes even as we speak, isolating the defective gene responsible for this tragic mental incapacity. And if getting a new name were free? Well, perhaps. But the library is free and Harris makes no use of that. Why? Who can say. Perhaps he has an outstanding fine for overdue books he is disinclined to pay. Or perhaps he's merely too busy lying in bed, lamenting and fretting.

Harris laments because he decided—when barely out of his teens—that he'd permanently ruined his chances in life, that he'd *blown it* (a favorite phrase). This conviction, though it results in much self-reproach and misery, rather conveniently absolves him from ever feeling obliged to *do* anything. He frets because he is a connoisseur of calamity, forever in a tizzy over some perceived threat to his well-being: deadly cell phone radiation, the inevitability of aging, suspicious neighbors, North Korean nukes, neurotoxic black mold spores—almost anything can set him off. He once phoned me from a laundromat in a total panic because a Swedish man was allegedly "glaring" at him with "malicious intent." Perhaps the only thing he *doesn't* fret about is the possibility that his fears might be nothing more than the mad fancies of a disordered mind.

Perhaps by now you can now guess why Harris fascinates me. He is at once an everyman, a one-of-a-kind oddity, a free-floating signifier, and an enigma wrapped in a riddle hidden in a jean jacket. He is a mental car crash from which I cannot look away. And he is undoubtedly *the* most annoying gay barfly in San Francisco. Yes, I am being judgmental, censorious, and perhaps even prosecutorial. What crime shall I eventually claim Harris is guilty of? I do not yet know—I only know that he is guilty. And what you cannot know, but should and must, is that Harris owes me ninety-two dollars and has *for quite some time.*

CHAPTER 2

INTRODUCING MAXINE

A RAMBUNCTIOUS YOUNG SCIENCE FICTION ENTHUSIAST once cornered me at a party and expounded at length about something called "string theory." Though somewhat inattentive due to mojitos, I gathered that physicists now suppose the universe to be composed of different strands of reality all bundled up like Armenian string cheese. I mention this because I'd like this story's narrative reality to shift strings, for a moment, to Harris's roommate, Maxine. Though pushing fifty, Maxine easily looked a decade younger, her gamine face and svelte figure having remained almost supernaturally free of wrinkles, sags, paunch, or bags. She liked to joke that because she was short, only five foot two, gravity had less to work with. A more plausible explanation is that she'd managed to mummify herself using some mysterious alchemy involving cigarettes, beer, and massive doses of raw ambition.

Maxine lived on the Social Security allowance for mental discombobulation and so her budget was limited.

Yet by intrepidly scouring thrift emporiums she'd scraped together a mid-century *femme fatale* wardrobe of swanky cocktail frocks, picture hats, and perilously high heels. She wore such clothes not only to nightclubs and bars, where they might plausibly be expected, but also to mundane locales such as the grocery store and the bank. So confident was her deportment and carriage, so unwavering her commitment to high glamour (she was, needless to say, a bottle blond), that hardly anyone noticed her clothes were full of small tears, often held together with visible safety pins, and possessed a lamentable tendency to molt, leaving behind a trail of feathers, sequins, and loose threads in her wake. There is an archaic English word, "flothery," meaning tawdry or slovenly but attempting to be fine and showy. I would like to resurrect it for immediate use. Maxine was ever so flothery.

When asked what she "did" (for people with jobs are always assuming that everyone else is so afflicted), Maxine called herself "an aspiring singer/songwriter." She'd been singing and writing songs through three decades, six presidencies, a sex change operation, and a couple of nervous breakdowns, but kept the "aspiring" to sound more like an ingénue. Her ultimate goal was to someday leverage her local celebrity into cult stardom. This hope, while far-fetched, was not irrational. Due to the pervasive prejudice against flamboyant, flothery people with nontraditional genders, Maxine was just as likely to be hailed as a Cabaret Phenomenon by the queer cognoscenti as hired to work at a shop or an office. Given the choice of longing for glorious fame or hoping for humble stability, she chose the former—as would, I imagine, you or I.

Our story begins one foggy, late summer afternoon in the fateful year of 1999 with Maxine traipsing along on fashionably bohemian Valencia Street wearing a tight satin cocktail dress of emerald green, gold strappy sandals, and some rather nice, orange Bakelite jewelry. Her hair was coiffed into a reasonable facsimile of the 'do worn by Barbara Stanwyck in the classic noir film *Double Indemnity* and over her shoulder hung a smart little black patent leather purse that wouldn't quite close due to being overfull. She'd just perused the shelves of Community Thrift and found nothing of interest and was looking for an excuse not to go home where Harris would likely be loafing about, a sight that tended to depress and annoy her.

As she crossed 17th Street, Maxine noticed a slender young man a few yards in front of her sporting a wild mane of hair bleached a dozen different shades of golden. He looked to be in the vicinity of twenty-one or twenty-two years old, an age Maxine found appealing. Thirsty for a better look, she quickened her pace. When the lad entered Muddy Waters, the least pretentious of the street's coffee shops, she followed him in, arriving just in time to see him turn away from the counter holding a steaming white ceramic mug.

On finally catching sight of the boy's face, Maxine realized he was none other than Jasper, who she'd recently met at an open mic for music at the Above Paradise. He'd performed some ballad with clever lyrics she couldn't recall, though she remembered vividly that he'd complimented her on her a cappella version of "Old Devil Moon." As at their first meeting, Jasper's delicate facial features dazzled Maxine, and she felt tempted to flirt. In days of yore, she wouldn't have bothered with a boy wearing, as Jasper was, pink sneakers on the grounds that he'd probably be homosexual. Nowadays, though, goofy clothes like Jasper's (he also wore plaid pants and a jeans jacket with a pigeon embroidered on the back) could as easily be the result of indie rock whimsy as gay camp.

Jasper managed to walk right by Maxine without noticing her on his way to a table. Once seated, he took a sip of his beverage and proceeded to stare straight ahead with a furiously concentrated look, as if entranced by a mystical apparition. "Oh, hello, Jasper!" sang out Maxine in a cheery falsetto, as if she'd just noticed him. He turned his head and faced her with a blank stare. She charged over to his table. "Having coffee?" she asked, seating herself across from him.

Startled, the boy sat upright. "Oh. Hi. Maxine, right?"

Maxine batted her lashes. "You were terrific the other night . . . with the song? You've got charisma. Did you know that?"

Jasper blushed adorably. "Thanks."

Maxine made her voice businesslike but tilted her head coquettishly. "You've got such sex appeal. All us girls in the audience were swooning." Jasper looked embarrassed, so she made a tactical retreat. "Hey, are you coming to my thing?"

Jasper's body recoiled reflexively. "Which *thing*?" he asked in a tone so wary as to border upon rudeness. Since everyone in Jasper's social set aspired to stardom in the creative arts, everyone was invited to far more *things* (film screenings, art openings, readings, plays, and musical gigs) than anyone could possibly attend. Even a moderately popular scenester might hear it three times a day. Are you coming to my thing? Are you coming to my thing? Are you coming to my thing? In consequence Jasper and everyone he knew continually suffered from a mixture of guilt over missing their friends's *things* and fear that their failure to attend said *things* would be interpreted as a snub and hence lead to someone skipping *their thing* in the future.

Despite his churlish response, Maxine gave Jasper her best sales pitch. "I'm doing a show next Monday at Big Louie's. Tickets are ten each, but I'll sell you two for one. You'll love it. Andy All Star's accompanying me on guitar now! This will be our third gig together and he's incredibly talented. Learns a song like that!" She snapped her fingers. "And he doesn't *noodle* the way so many guitarists do, just to show you how talented they are. Our press release describes his style as spare and witty."

"You gotta work with the right people," opined Jasper, nodding sagely.

"Of course, I still need a drummer, bassist, and maybe someone on sax or trumpet, but for all that I'd need a backer." Maxine smiled winningly. "Are you by any chance a trust fund baby with a few thousand dollars to invest?"

"Nuh-uh," said Jasper, vigorously shaking his head.

"No stocks? No bonds? No family jewels? You sure your grandmother didn't leave fifty-thousand dollars for you in a trust somewhere?" Maxine's tone was light and bantering, yet Jasper looked startled as if he'd discovered someone rifling through his wallet.

"Starving student."

"Oh well. It's only a matter of time before I find someone. I've got a killer set now. I do the Supremes's 'Living in Shame,' Terry Jacks's 'Seasons in the Sun,' and I just added 'Little Willie' by the Sweet. I used to do 'Little Willie' with this drag troupe the Summer Campers. God, that was centuries ago . . ."

"The *Summer Campers*?" echoed Jasper, scowling.

"Oh I know, I know, it was a *terrible* name," said Maxine contritely, sitting on her hands. "But they were drag queens: tacky, tacky drag queens. I was the only R.G. in the bunch. That's R.G. for real girl, which compared to those tired queens I was, though at that point I wasn't even on hormones yet. Actually, the minute you start changing your sex all the professionals tell you to keep away from the drag scene, but I think that's so old fashioned. There're lots of natural born females who do drag these days, they're called faux queens."

Jasper nodded. "Sure, sure."

"Anyways, the whole point of the Summer Campers was to be awful. But 'Little Willie' is a fabulous song. It's dirty. Get it? Little Willie? Just come to the show. I'll get you a drink ticket too."

"I don't drink," said Jasper.

Maxine was struck dumb.

Jasper put on a non-threatening smile. "Just not my thing. I mean, no judgments or whatever."

Maxine rummaged through her overfull purse. "How about one ticket for five bucks? You'll love the space too, a real old-fashioned dive with Deco fixtures behind the bar and . . . ah, here we are!" She extracted a Xeroxed rectangle of pink card stock and slapped it on the wobbly table between them, causing a bit of coffee to slosh over the side of Jasper's mug.

Jasper put on a helpless face. "I have, like, zero dollars."

Maxine sighed. "Oh, just be there. I'll put you on the guest list." She paused, smiling slyly. "You know, you don't have to be broke all the time. You could make a *mint* turning tricks as a lady-boy. That face! That figure! You should let me fix you up and take you to out."

"I don't think so," said Jasper, sounding a trifle alarmed.

Maxine batted her lashes again. "Oh, I shouldn't suggest such a *wicked* thing, you're a *nice* boy, aren't you?"

"Not hardly," said Jasper, now a trifle offended. "Hey, are you going to the Velveteen Sporks at Club 69? I'm go-go dancing."

Maxine felt validated that Jasper, nearly two decades her junior, would feel she was hip enough to be invited to his *thing.* "I haven't decided yet," said Maxine, who'd never heard of the Velveteen Sporks and had no intention of going. "I used to play Club 69," she added, because it was true and she could.

"Right on," said Jasper. (Readers need scarcely be told this was not the baby boomer *right on* with the accent on the second word and meaning "Viva Che, LSD, and paisley bell bottoms!" but the generation X *right on* with the accent on the first word and meaning "that's nice.")

Feeling that her mission, such as it was, had been accomplished, Maxine stood up to leave. "Nice seeing you Jasper, but I should be getting home. Toodles!"

Jasper gave a little wave. "Yah. *Toodles!*"

Maxine couldn't tell if the tone of Jasper's "toodles" was sarcastic, meaning he thought she was uncool for using such archaic slang, or ironic, meaning he'd understood *she* was using the word ironically and was paying homage through appropriation. Why did young people have to be so difficult?

CHAPTER 3

EXPELLED

MAXINE ARRIVED AT HER APARTMENT BUILDING at Post and Larkin and rode the slow, rickety birdcage of an elevator to the fourth floor. As she stood in the mildew-smelling hallway outside her door rummaging through her purse for her keys she heard, faintly, Harris talking on the phone inside.

". . . No, I don't have anything *particular* to say, but since you never seem to be able to find the time to call me . . . I *know* you're busy with Dad . . . I *know* osteoporosis is no picnic . . . I *understand* that . . . Look, did I ask to be brought into this world? Is it too much to ask that . . . Well, maybe I should just pretend I *have* no mother . . ."

Maxine realized with twinge of shame that she was eavesdropping but knew that if she went inside Harris would likely clam up. She pressed her ear to the door.

"Money? Why should I be asking for money? Being destitute is a blast, a non-stop party . . . What *do* I *want* from you? How about being a *mother*? There's a novel idea. Correct me if I'm wrong, but I think parents are supposed to be supportive . . . And now with this Y2K thing coming up . . . Y2K, you must have heard of it . . . Well, it seems the *geniuses* who programmed all these computers that now *run our lives*, whether we like it or not, didn't think about the first two digits of the year changing from 19 to 20. So the computers don't have the capacity to even, I don't know, *compute* that the year two thousand is even a possibility. Come January first these so-called *thinking machines* will *think* we're in the year zero-zero and, who knows, maybe just shut off! And nowadays computers run *everything*. Streetlights, phones, banks, the government . . ."

There was a long pause.

"Oh come now, Mother, you're too smart for that. I mean, here I am, trapped in this hideous city . . . I don't care what you've read. San Francisco is a cesspool! What's more, I'm in the Tenderloin, the *worst* part of town in a tiny, *scuzzy* apartment with a crazy roommate who's . . ."

Before Harris could finish his sentence, adrenalized fury propelled Maxine into the apartment where she beheld Harris sprawled out on the living room sofa, which doubled as his bed, phone receiver in one hand, lit cigarette in the other.

Harris modulated his voice in an effort to sound unworried. "Mom? Something's come up. I'll have to call you back later. Bye." Harris gingerly hung up the phone. "Hi Maxine, what's up?"

Maxine slammed the door shut behind her. "Crazy?"

Harris flashed what he hoped was an appeasing smile. "I was speaking with my mother and . . . uh, I . . ."

Maxine all but shrieked, "You think I'm *crazy?*"

"Of course not! I was, uh . . ."

"You're pathetic," interrupted Maxine. She went into the kitchenette, grabbed a beer from the fridge, and returned to the living room where she perched on the armchair opposite Harris and glowered. "Why can't you leave that poor woman alone?" She popped open the beer and took a swallow.

"My mother and I have a complicated relationship. I wouldn't expect you to understand." Unsure what to do with his eyes, Harris stared at the collage he'd made from glossy magazines of inspirational celebrities that hung on the wall to the right of his sofa: Diana Vreeland, John Sex, Vivienne Westwood, Quentin Crisp, Nancy Sinatra, Sophia Loren, Bryan Ferry, and Lovey Howell from *Gilligan's Island.*

Maxine continued her assault, her fury intensifying with every breath. "You're a grown man. Take some responsibility. Why should some old woman in Florida care if you're happy or not? Instead of sitting around on your ass feeling *sorry* for yourself go find a better job or enroll in community college or, I don't know, clean the fucking bathroom. Just do *something* instead of being a professional pain in the ass!"

"You're out of control," said Harris, nervously stabbing out his cigarette in the 1950's pink porcelain candy dish they used for an ashtray.

"Whose?" Maxine asked in a cold fury.

"Whose, what?" asked Harris, continuing to grind the cigarette with a malevolence it had clearly not earned all by itself.

"Whose control am I out of?" elucidated Maxine with a tight little smile. "Yours?"

"I'm only pointing out—" said Harris, finally releasing the cigarette butt, "—what any good friend would: that you have crossed a line . . ." He hesitated, then adopted the breathy Southern drawl of a Tennessee Williams heroine while fanning himself with a postcard he found lying on the coffee table. "Crossed the perilously thin line between sanity and being, shall we say, *unwell.*"

Maxine stood up. "So you *do* think I'm crazy!"

"For heaven's sake! I'm joking! Lighten up!"

"And speaking of the rent, you still owe me fifteen dollars."

"But I *did* give you three-ten on the first."

"Yes, and your share of the rent is three-twenty-five. I still haven't paid half the rent for August because of you! By rights I could ask you to leave *right now.*"

"I certainly can't see a compassionate person like yourself evicting someone over a mere fifteen dollars!"

"So you'll be able to give me the fifteen *and* the three-twenty-five on September first with no problem?"

Harris reflexively glanced at his calendar. It was Friday, August 27. "Of course! Sure! I mean, maybe not right *on* the first as I don't get paid until *the following* Friday . . ."

Maxine resisted a strong urge to throttle Harris. Throwing out roommates was never easy, but Harris had been working her nerves for months now and she was in a mood. "I would like you," she said, enunciating the words carefully to increase their menace, "To remove yourself from these premises. I want every trace of you gone by midnight August 31st." Harris peered at her in silence, his face an ashen white. "Do you hear me?" She leaned toward him and lowered her voice to a menacing whisper. "I want you to move out." The silence that followed seemed to contain an echo: *move out, move out, move out.*

Had Maxine been shrieking mid-tantrum, Harris would have dismissed this eviction notice as part of a temporary derangement. Her eerie calm, however, suggested she meant business. There was still the slim possibility this was part of some nasty mind-game. Maxine was, after all, a highly theatrical person. He tried to sound her out. "Surely you can't mean that. Here we've been living together, for the most part peaceably, for *over* a year. I can't imagine you would suddenly . . ."

"During that year," interrupted Maxine, sitting back down and smoothing her dress with an agitated gesture, "You have been late with the rent nearly every single month, you have criticized my decorating skills . . ."

"Well, it's criminal the way you have a room all to your own, not a mere couch in a living room as I'm forced to make do with, and you've never fixed it up! I mean, *please,* using a milk crate as a nightstand is understandable if you're a nineteen-year-old Goth chick with a pet rat, but you're a mature woman."

"I can't *believe* you just said that."

"I don't mean mature like *old,* I mean like *sophisticated.*"

"Also, you have insulted my houseguests . . ."

"That piece of rough trade you brought home was going through my belongings!"

Maxine's eyes took on the malevolent cast of a cat about to dismember a mouse. "The fact is that I don't like you. I have never liked you. I hate you. I despise you." She stood again and folded her arms in a display of social dominance. "The lease is in my name, this is my apartment, and I want you out of here on the first."

"Maxine, be reasonable. It's customary to give a month's notice! I'll get the rent. All of it and I won't be late! I give you my word as a gentleman!"

Maxine manufactured a short bitter laugh then thrust her face within a few inches of Harris' and stage whispered. "You better not make me any madder than I already am. You don't know what I might do. Remember I'm *craaaazy.*"

On some level Maxine was clearly playacting, but on another level she was also (he deduced from the unblinking intensity of her widened eyes) quite serious. Zombified with confusion, frustration, and terror, Harris rose from his seat, grabbed a jacket, and marched himself out of the apartment.

CHAPTER 4

INTRODUCING WALLY

As he walked in the general direction of nowhere, Harris considered his options. There was no way could he get a place of his own as even skid row studios were suddenly renting for a king's ransom thanks to the influx of computer savvy youngsters cashing in on the dot-com boom. True, there were residence hotels where one could pay by the week, but on a monthly basis they were just as expensive as apartments, as well as filthy, smelly, crime-ridden, and prone to burning down in mysterious fires after which gleaming million-dollar lofts invariably rose in their place. No, he'd just have to find someone with a cheap, rent-controlled apartment who'd let him move in (and without demanding anything so vile as last month's rent and/or a security deposit). He scoured his mind for candidates and came up with only one name: Wally.

A cherubic, bedimpled thirty-one-year-old wisecracker, Wally was a devotee of extreme tastelessness, prone to wearing amusingly passé clothes from the 1970s: loudly patterned polyester shirts, over-large sunglasses, wide ties and the like. His get-ups managed to look clever rather than clownish only because Wally sincerely loved these fashion relics and wore them with more élan than irony. He worked at Kinko's, a copy shop, and devoted his free time to his theater company, which produced stage parodies of old movies and television, heavy on cross-dressing and raunchy innuendo. He and Harris had forged their camaraderie over the course of a thousand nights (yes, literally a thousand) spent drinking together at various disreputable taverns.

Wally paid a modest rent to live in a vast, ramshackle Victorian flat in the Haight with a bevy of slacker roommates. Flats like this were something of a San Francisco specialty. Designed for 19th century extended families and their servants, they now served as dorm-like housing for young hipsters and deadbeats. Such households tended to be noisy, messy, and overcrowded, but turnover rates were high as someone was always moving away to attend film school or start a new life in Portland. Harris determined to investigate the possibility immediately and set out for Wally's.

After a brisk walk to Market Street, Harris stood shivering at the bus stop along with a few office drones. He glanced into the street but saw no bus. Resigning himself to a long wait, his mind ran through a litany of despair: *Wally probably won't want me to move in because I'm a loser. Maxine is a creep, and I'm a loser for knowing her. My parents think I'm a loser and won't help me now and never will. It's freezing cold. Everyone hates me. The Mayor and the city government are totally corrupt. I'm ugly. I'm short. I'm* gay. *I'm poor. I'll never find true love. The new generation has been morally corrupted by gangsta rap or infantilized by insipid boy bands . . .*

Eventually the bus arrived. *Stuffed with the dregs of humanity,* Harris thought to himself as he boarded. MUNI, San Francisco's streetcar/bus system, is utterly (one is tempted to say thankfully) unique. Have you ever had a washing machine that jiggles so much that it moves forward a few inches with each use? This same principle is behind the propulsion system for MUNI busses. Even short rides are liable to displace one's internal organs through sheer vibration. And of course, the term "short" when applied to MUNI is relative. Due to the city's perpetually gridlocked traffic, unscheduled coffee breaks (during which the driver abandons the bus, disappears into a convenience store, and returns five minutes later laughing over some joke with the proprietor), technical difficulties involving streetcar wires, and altercations amongst the passengers during which the bus must sit still as the driver demands that the culprits take their squabble outside, it takes very nearly *forever* to get anywhere.

Eventually, though, the bus did deposit Harris at the corner of Haight and Cole. He'd only taken a few steps when one of a pair of longhaired teens dressed in patched jeans and tie-dye sitting cross-legged on the sidewalk called out to him. "Hey, got any spare change?"

Catching sight of their psychedelic tatters, Harris bristled. "The Summer of Love was over thirty years ago. *Why* are you dressed like that?"

The kids dissolved into stoned laughter and Harris scurried away. Soon enough he found himself at Wally's flat, the first floor of a decrepit multi-family Victorian. He walked up the steps to the porch and lit a cigarette to calm his nerves. Then he rang the bell. After a long moment, Wally's roommate Ted opened the door.

"Fetching ensemble," said Harris. Ted was clad in denim cut-offs and a faded Pixies t-shirt. "Is grunge making a come-back *already*?" He waited a beat as if expecting a witty rejoinder, but Ted stood mutely, staring with horror at the lit cigarette in Harris's hand. "The customary thing to do when someone rings your bell is ask him in. Or am I expected to stand here on your welcome mat all night?"

"Hey Harris. Sure, come on in . . . but this is a non-smoking household. You can't smoke in here."

Harris rolled his eyes. "Darling, I *know* you can't smoke in a non-smoking household. Be that as it may, I've only just lit up, so give me a second, if that's not asking *too* terribly much." He inhaled deeply then turned his head to exhale the smoke away from the door. Ted stood waiting. Harris took another puff. Ted shifted his weight from one foot to the other. "I'm here to see Wally," said Harris, just to be polite. After all, Ted would soon be his roommate if everything went according to plan.

"Figured," said Ted.

"One more puff." Harris inhaled once more then dropped his butt out on the stoop and, ignoring Ted's horrified glare, stamped it out.

"He's in the kitchen," said Ted.

Harris entered the hallway exhaling a huge cloud of smoke. "I know the way."

Ted fled into his bedroom as Harris made his way to the kitchen where he discovered Wally seated at a Formica table in front of a giant mixing bowl. Harris peered in the bowl and frowned in disgust at a giant mass of florescent orange noodles shaped like dinosaurs.

"What're you eating?" asked Harris.

"Dino mac 'n' cheese."

"Why?"

"Uh . . . 'cause I'm hungry?"

Harris sat across from his friend. "Could you dim the lights? This kitchen is filthy."

"I cleaned it two days ago," said Wally. He rose and flipped off the overheads so that the room was illuminated only by a strand of colored Christmas lights strung around windows.

"You need to clean again," insisted Harris. "Or are you too butch for housework?"

"We have a lot of people living here, it gets dirty quickly."

"Correct me if I'm wrong, but that also means you also have a lot of people to clean."

Just then Wally's adorable roommate Casey popped his head into the kitchen. "Hey, my friend Cecil's coming over. He rented *Jurassic Park*, you guys wanna watch?"

"No thanks," said Wally. "I hate computer-generated special effects."

"Darling, we don't need to *watch* dinosaurs, we *are* dinosaurs," drawled Harris.

As Wally cackled, Casey shrugged. "Okay. Well, you know where to find me if you change your mind." He left the room.

"So what brings you here?" asked Wally.

Harris folded his hands on the table in an effort to appear businesslike. "I came to talk to you about an opportunity."

"Go on."

Harris smiled sweetly. "This might be best discussed over libations." Wally rose and pulled a pair of *Flintstones* jelly jars out of a cupboard. "Only alcoholics drink out of jars. Don't you have hi-ball glasses?"

"What do you think?" asked Wally. He poured some vodka from a conveniently located economy-sized bottle then plopped in a few ice cubes from the freezer.

Harris winced. "You should put the ice in first and pour the booze *over* it. Tastes better that way. Don't ask me why, but it does."

Wally sighed. "Anything else, princess?"

"What are we using for mixer?"

Wally took a bottle of grape juice from the fridge and splashed a bit into the jars. "Voila! Purple Jesuses."

"Is this something you learned at college?" asked Harris with a dubious look. He ruefully sipped his drink and winced as if in pain. "Well, the thing is. . . As I said, there's an opportunity for you. And it involves me." He paused for another sip.

"Okay, go on . . ."

"I think this could be really good for both of us. A golden opportunity."

"Yes, an opportunity. Got it. Got it."

"Honey, take a chill pill!" admonished Harris. "Or at least have some of your drink. You're all wound up"

"Just spit it out!"

"Fine." Harris took a gulp of his drink and continued. "I may have the solution to all your housing problems."

"What housing problems?"

"Well, you know how you're always complaining about your roommates not cleaning up and being late with the rent and all that?"

"I'm not *always* complaining about that. In fact, I *never* complain about that."

"Well, I have the solution. It's really a great opportunity. . ."

"Get to the point!"

"You *really* need to do something about your nerves. Well, as I said, there's an opportunity in that Maxine and I have had a little contretemps and I may be looking for somewhere to move. So . . ."

Wally cut him off. "We don't have a spare bedroom right now."

"I thought maybe one of those no accounts you live with might be moving out."

"Nope."

"But the lease is in your name, am I right?"

"Yeah. But I can't throw someone out for no reason."

"I'm not asking you to throw anyone out. You could give them notice and I'd sleep on the sofa in the living room till they left."

"The thing is," said Wally, speaking in the hesitant manner of someone who suspects he's being foolhardy, "We used to rent out the back porch but stopped because that guy Pierre was such a pain and we all decided there wasn't really room for five people here."

"This place is huge," said Harris.

"But it only has one bathroom," countered Wally.

"I promise I won't spend more than fifteen minutes a day in there," said Harris.

"It takes you fifteen minutes just to style your eyebrows."

"Wouldn't it be nice to split the rent five ways again?"

Wally stared off into the distance as if ogling a pile of cash. "Well, yeah. But there *are* other issues."

"Such as?"

"Smoking."

"Well, I won't smoke in the house," said Harris.

"And I hate to bring it up . . ."

"Then don't."

"But you're a mooch! You're constantly coming over here and drinking my booze. You're a hooch-mooch!"

"Well, if I lived here you could drink all *my* booze. And think," Harris added in a business-y tone. "You'll have an extra . . . what am I going to be paying?"

"Pierre was paying two seventy-five," said Wally.

"You'll have an extra two hundred seventy-five dollars *every month*!" Harris pondered the figure. "Really? Two seventy-five for a tiny unheated back porch next to the water heater? It's not even really a room."

"Welcome to the '90s."

"Well, okay," said Harris.

Though Wally's conscious mind was frantically waving red flags, his unconscious mind firmly associated Harris with the joys of inebriation and was all in favor of his moving in. "It could be kinda fun. We could have parties . . ."

"Like the one in *Breakfast at Tiffany's*!"

At the mention of his favorite film, Wally's expression changed from unsure to resolved. "Okay. Let me talk it over with my roommates."

"Great," said Harris. "But remember, you're the *master* tenant."

"Hey," said Wally. "My play's closing Sunday and you haven't been yet, have you?"

"I was planning to go Sunday," lied Harris. "Closing night is always the best performance. Any chance you could put me on the guest list?"

Wally sighed. His shows generally played to packed (if tiny) houses, but he never made a dime because so many people insisted on being comped. "I guess."

"Great, I'll see you then if not before." As Harris rose to leave, he glanced around the kitchen. "Once I move in, I'll help you redecorate. It's really a crime how you've never bothered to fix this place up."

CHAPTER 5

MAXINE HATCHES A PLOT

Maxine grabbed another beer from the fridge and retreated to what she liked to call her "boudoir." She collapsed on her bed and replayed the story of meeting Harris on the silver screen of her memory. They'd met in line at the DMV when Harris complimented her pink paillette-sequined mini-frock. In the course of an hour's chat, they discovered a shared love of low camp and high modernism, Fellini, hashish, old Bowie, and New Orleans. Furthermore, they both loathed reggae, Los Angeles, Elton John, and LSD. Being so brilliantly simpatico called for a celebration, so after completing their mundane business at the DMV they went cocktailing in North Beach. The hours and drinks flew by and at the end of the night, drunk as spring break frat rats, they collapsed on Maxine's queen-sized bed sharing a bottle of cognac and the intimate details of their respective childhoods.

The next morning, cotton-mouthed and grouchy, they'd gone out for coffee. The café was blasting Hole's "Teenage Whore" at stadium volume and Harris had started an argument by claiming Courtney Love was responsible for Kurt's death. "It's the same story as Nancy Spungen and Sid Vicious. A talentless tramp uses her dubious sex appeal to ruin a great star."

"What?" scoffed Maxine. "Kurt shot *himself.* Sid *killed* Nancy."

"Well," Harris snipped, "I think it might behoove you to rethink your position. I mean, who brought what to those relationships? Correct me if I'm wrong, but Sid and Kurt brought talent, Nancy and Courtney brought only drugs."

"I cannot sit here and listen to you slander the genius that is Courtney Love," said Maxine, setting down her mug and rising to her full five-two. "Leave now, or I shall be forced to destroy you." Harris left.

Despite its reputation as an actual city, San Francisco is actually a wee hamlet of forty-seven square miles. Within its tiny confines everyone runs into everyone else sooner or later, usually sooner. Thus, it's not surprising that a mere two months after their argument Maxine ran into Harris at Cafe Flore, a woodsy, windowed place with lots of outdoor seating, plants, and a hip queer clientele given to table hopping. Harris, who'd just received his tax refund, was feeling flush and treating himself to a luxurious breakfast of waffles and champagne. Though still irritated by Maxine's wrong opinions, Harris feared that drinking alone in public before noon made him look alcoholic. Thus, seeing her join the line for ordering at the long, old-fashioned wooden bar, beckoned her over. "Miss Maxine, what a pleasant surprise!"

After a moment's hesitation, Maxine decided to respond as if Harris were an old friend. She bestowed a pair of air kisses in his general direction and sat herself down at his tiny table. As they traded introductory pleasantries, she poured herself a glass of bubbly using an empty water glass and used Harris's salad fork to start in on his French toast.

"Go ahead and finish," said Harris. "It's not very good." He pushed the plate across the table. "I should have ordered the eggs Benedict, but I can't really face the . . . well, I'm not even going to dignify it by calling it Hollandaise sauce, I'm sure it comes out of a *can* or something, let's just say, I don't care for that *substance* they put on it here. I mean, the color is somewhere between ecru and . . ."

Hoping to forestall further discussion of the Hollandaise, Maxine interrupted. "I rented this incredible movie the other night, *Night of The Hunter* . . ."

Harris squealed like a teenybopper. "That movie is *soooo* amazing!" Within minutes Maxine was feigning agreement with Harris's extensive cultural litmus test: The Beatles, no! Sparks, yes! Large dogs, no! The city of Chicago, no! Sushi, yes! Cranberry colored hair, no! Germans, no! Tiki bars, yes! Truman Capote, yes! The 1980s, no! Small New England towns, yes! (Here we must bear witness to the fact that Harris's litmus test was not totally arbitrary; for the most part he simply disdained anything popular, vulgar, masculine, anti-intellectual, self-serious, or contemporary in favor of the recherché, sophisticated, feminine, clever, campy, and antiquated. All in all, not the worst system one could imagine.)

Before long, validated and tipsy, Harris decided that he'd been hasty in dismissing Maxine. She was actually rather delightful! Maxine, in turn, was fascinated by the way Harris's face glowed with pleasure each time he discovered a shared view, as if it were a personal victory that another human being detested chili dogs or worshipped Sal Mineo. For the sake of verisimilitude (how likely is it that two people would agree on everything?) she tried expressing a divergent opinion, saying she wasn't a huge fan of Doris Day. With a hurt look in his eyes and cold venom in his voice Harris muttered, "I suppose you buy into the *conventional* wisdom that she's too plastic or something." Maxine quickly backtracked. On second thought she *had* always liked Doris in *The Pajama Game.* Harris smiled with satisfaction. Maxine only had to agree with him a couple more times before her transgression was forgotten.

Within an hour, Maxine had casually mentioned that she was in a bit of a pickle because her bitch of a roommate had left without notice after a silly fight over Maxine borrowing some of her food. As it happened, Harris was looking for cheaper digs himself. Aided by good vibes from their pleasant conversation and a full bottle of champagne, this coincidence struck both of them as positively cosmic. Clearly fate had brought them together! It was quickly agreed that Harris would move in posthaste.

Once he'd settled in, Maxine recruited Harris into her

never-ending quest for stardom. The pair began with long boozy discussions of cabaret and musical theater, and before long Maxine was demanding advice on songs, outfits, hairstyles, and press releases, all of which Harris gave unstintingly. Why he felt her clip-on chignon was absolutely right for one performance or absolutely wrong for another was never entirely clear, but she found it nice to have someone with whom to discuss the matter as if the fate of the universe hinged upon the decision. She also enjoyed the way Harris would flutter around her before shows, helping find wayward earrings, fixing preparatory cocktails, and—when it was time to leave—toting cigarettes, throat lozenges, and other essentials to the gig in his man purse. And it was fun how Harris disparaged her competition, calling the tall, doe-eyed, and slender Randi Riviera "a praying mantis in drag," or averring that Maria Martini's voice was so hoarse it oughta wear a saddle. (Please note: although they cackled at such bitchery, Harris and Maxine actually quite liked Randi and Maria.) That he clearly adored her performances was icing on the cake and she grew to rely on him as her lady-in-waiting.

On the other hand, Harris generally wasn't much fun until sundown. During the day he tended to be terse and moody. True, he was tidy, but she was constantly forced to haggle with him over money. He was always late with the rent and acted not just surprised but insulted by the arrival of the utility bill each month, as if Pacific Gas & Electric were an estranged relative who'd suddenly asked for a loan. Equally annoying, there was a noticeable coldness in his demeanor after she entertained gentlemen callers. It was anyone's guess whether this was due to rank jealousy (Harris never had callers of his own) or his generalized squeamishness around sex. Lady-in-waiting or not, Harris could still be a giant pain in the ass.

To avoid further thoughts of Harris, Maxine grabbed yet another beer and turned on the portable TV she'd found in her neighbor's trash. The reception was atrocious, but through the blizzard on screen she could just make out five presumably attractive young people eating pizza. The sound was clear enough, and for several minutes she listened, growing more disgusted with each burst of canned laughter. When a svelte girl went into a long self-depreciating riff on dieting Maxine completely lost her temper. "One more word about being overweight from you Miss Toothpick and I'll fly to Hollywood and eat you!" She shut off the TV.

With nothing else to do, Maxine fell back on her go-to activity: self-promotion. She picked up the phone and dialed Brian, the proprietor of Club 69. She and Brian had slept together a few times, slightly over a decade ago, and for a few years thereafter he'd occasionally booked her as an opening act.

Brian answered on the first ring with a terse, "Yeah?"

"Brian, it's Maxine!"

"Oh, Maxi. Hi."

"Hey, I wanted to give you a little ringy-dingy 'cause I'm touring again! I'm playing next Monday at Big Louie's, just to get kinda warmed up, and then I was thinking I might make myself available for some shows at Club 69."

"You know, Maxi, the club's been getting a real young crowd lately. Bridge and tunnel mostly. I just don't think they'd get your act."

Maxine knew this to be true. Suburban types went out to blast off and stop thinking. They found her set of pop gems from decades past too obscure and her clever stage patter wearying. She was not, however, one to give up easily. "Brian, what makes San Francisco magical is how it's always so mixed-up and inappropriate and unexpected. Having a classy chanteuse like *moi* sing for a bunch of suburbanites is mixed-up and inappropriate and unexpected. It's your civic duty to book me!"

"No can do, babe."

Maxine knew what the issue was. Even when straight crowds didn't clock her as trans, which wasn't often, her attitude toward gender was too playfully *recherché* for them. Guys positively squirmed when she called them "big butch things" or asked them to "show Miss Maxi some muscle" and gals were perplexed by her devotion to all the vampish accouterments—five-inch spike heels, girdles, false eyelashes—they couldn't be bothered with. She might've gotten away with it if she'd played for laughs, like a drag queen, but Maxine's shtick was sincerely and brazenly sexual.

"You know, if you always cater to the lowest common denominator you'll eventually lose your hipster cachet. It's not even good business!"

"Sorry Maxi. Try me again around like. . . maybe closer to Halloween."

"Halloween?" For a brief second Maxine was so consumed with rage that all words fled her mind in terror. When, after a few seconds, she calmed down enough that they dared creep back, she spat, "You're *ugly* and I *hate* you and I hope you die of some *terrible disease!*" She slammed down the phone. Rather than smash something in anger (a distinct possibility) she marched into the kitchen to get herself a third beer. In doing so she caught sight of Harris's empty couch. Ugh! Throwing him out had been fun, but now she'd have to find someone to replace him—and in a hurry, too.

Past roommates (there had been six in the five years she'd lived there) had always come from friends' recommendations. As Maxine sprawled across Harris's couch and guzzled her beer, she recalled that the papers were full of horror stories about the exorbitant rents everyone was suddenly paying due to something called "the dot-com boom." Maybe (just maybe!) she could find someone to pay a good bit more than Harris. Four hundred? Four fifty? Five? Why not? A delicious frisson of excitement tingled her entire body. She was about to become fabulously, gloriously rich!

CHAPTER 6

A LITTLE MORE ABOUT HARRIS

HARRIS IS A MYSTERIOUS AND IMPROBABLE character, yet by mixing personal observations with anecdotal evidence and wild speculation I believe it possible to create a roughly accurate picture of his typical day. Though this description lies in that gray area betwixt gossip and infotainment, I advise readers against dismissing it as mere literary fabrication. Post-modernists employed for hefty salaries by top universities have declared that truth is subjective and unknowable; thus, my conjectures are surely as close to so-called "reality" as anything else.

Now, from approximately 3 a.m. to 3 p.m., Harris tries to sleep. His mind seethes and frets as he twists around on his sofa-bed trying to get comfortable until his body is splayed out like someone who's fallen from a great height. He tries counting sheep, then regrets, but before sleep takes hold a thought, unbidden yet unavoidable, occurs: *I could die during the night.* He curls into a fetal position and wraps himself tightly with the blanket in the vain hope of creating a comforting, womb-like effect.

Death conjures no thoughts of heavenly peace for Harris, only the image of his own corpse, naked and sallow on a marble slab and the overwhelming sense of having been cheated. How miserly life had been with its pleasures! He'd had no whirlwind trips to Rome, no torrid summer romances with boys half his age, no personality profiles in the newspaper's Sunday style section. Rather, his life had been an endless cycle of drudgery and humiliation. And with his bad luck, the future would surely be just as rotten. He'd likely be mowed down by some yuppie's speeding SUV, if not slain and devoured by cannibalistic bandits during the anarchy following the collapse of society after Y2K. Certain of an imminent and tragic demise, Harris stretches out flat on his back and folds his arms over his chest in funereal fashion. This is oddly soothing, and he drifts into a dreamy sleep-like state in which his monstrous terrors and even more monstrous desires can tango through his psyche unhindered by reason or good taste. He is, in his fashion, at rest.

At three in the afternoon, Harris's alarm goes off, rousing him with its annoying buzz. He lies still for a moment in a state of shock, thinking: *Not again. Not another day on this wretched planet with these tedious people.* He sits up, blinks, stretches, yawns, rises to his feet, and heads into the bathroom. Before leaving the apartment, Harris requires approximately ninety minutes of uninterrupted grooming. The first half of this is taken up with a long, hot, steamy shower, the application of innumerable unguents, creams, and lotions, and the buffing of his nails. The second half is devoted to the combing, teasing, and finally, moussing of his hair. For those unacquainted with it, hair mousse is a foamy and completely ineffectual styling product that enjoyed a brief vogue during the 1980s but which has now been largely forgotten, except by Harris who is devoted to it. Does he sport a complicated 'do, a rockabilly waterfall, a faux-hawk, or one of those geometrical oddities made famous by Vidal Sassoon? No, Harris has the standard hair of a high school science teacher or state senator. *Nothing* hair. One could ask why it takes so long to style it, but one might as well ask why light travels at 186,000 miles per second. Nobody really knows.

Once out of the house, Harris purchases a decaf tea from a nearby cafe. Caffeine makes him jittery and he denounces it at every opportunity as "nothing more than legalized crank." After that he heads to work at McWhitty Market Research, a "boiler room" operation where he conducts phone interviews from 5:30 to 9:30 p.m., Sunday through Thursday. The only qualifications for working there are a mastery of standard English and the ability to withstand torturous levels of boredom. You'll hear more about it later, so with your kind indulgence I'll skip ahead.

After work, Harris faces the trauma of eating. He doesn't require much in the way of sustenance. One full meal a day will satisfy him. The problem is, Harris finds most foods so unappetizing he can barely force them down his gullet. When he can afford to, he dines out, but often his budget will not extend beyond the self-serve salad bar at upmarket health food stores or some fancy cheese and a baguette. You see, Harris looks to the *status* inherent in a meal to nourish him rather than the nutrients. Every upscale bite associates him (albeit only on a symbolic level) with people who drive sporty cars, visit wineries, and enjoy retirement plans. He chews slowly, like a cow in a pasture, savoring not the taste, but the delicious social implications of his repasts.

Harris much prefers smoking to eating. It is something he's very good at. He pays particular attention to the *art* of smoking, the *chic* of it. Harris cannot do anything else while smoking. He will stand with his weight on one hip like a fashion model, fold his arms over his chest like a movie star, and go at it. Puff, puff, puff. Once he's finished his postprandial cigarette, it will be time to get ready to go out. Harris is dedicated to the magic and mystery of *nightlife*, a real Party Person.

For those uninitiated with the concept of being a Party Person, allow me to explain.

For millennia, human existence consisted of ceaseless labor relieved only by the occasional orgy of pointless bloodshed. Life was not only "short, nasty, and brutish," but dirty, dull, and disappointing. Relief from this endless misery came only from parties. Weddings, births, military victories, holy days, and harvests each merited a celebration during which our wretched forebears could forget their woes and cathartically release tension through intoxication, flirting, and the enjoyment of finger foods. This state of affairs lasted from the first caveman barbecues honoring successful mastodon hunts until about 1964 when the sixties really started to *swing*. At that time a paradigm shift occurred in human consciousness making it possible to have a party that wasn't celebrating anything, a party for its own sake.

Now, some scholars contend that the party-for-its-own-sake was invented by *fin de siècle* French decadents, others insist on the Roaring Twenties. Whatever the case, it wasn't until the advent of Swinging London, Warhol's Factory, and the Summer of Love that the idea of the party as *lifestyle* came into its own. Now, the sixties, as we all know from various tell-all memoirs and "behind-the-music" documentaries, came to a tragic end with people choking to death in their own vomit and such. But as with women's lib and flared trousers, the trend of partying for its own sake survived the great meltdown.

Like all revolutions, though, the party revolution produced militant partisans who pushed things *too far*. First, they transmogrified the perfectly nice noun, *party*, into the slightly sinister verb, *partying*. Following that, they completely conquered and occupied Palm Springs, Fort Lauderdale, and the formerly idyllic Mediterranean isle of Ibiza. In San Francisco, these "Party People" consolidated their power base in the SOMA district and quickly spread to the Mission, Castro, Tenderloin, North Beach, and points beyond. By 1999 the only thing keeping the entire northeastern quadrant of the city from descending into a state of perpetual revelry was the overworked, understaffed noise abatement squad of the SFPD.

Once out on the town, Harris really comes alive. Between eleven-ish and when the bars close at 2 a.m., party time, his social genius shines. By turns he is a flattering sycophant, heaping praise upon a deejay while shamelessly begging for drink tickets; a gossip extraordinaire, spreading malicious rumors with an air of disingenuous compassion; and a surprisingly clever conversationalist, full of witty repartee and astute comments. He will always have a tip on the best new bands, the hottest new fashion designers, and the wildest new gossip. On top of that, his outfits are memorably fashion-forward, and he is even a good dancer. If it weren't for his lackluster hair, one might almost declare Harris the Perfect Party Person.

Now, most sensitive reader, I sense your unease. You are not sure you wish to use your precious reading time to delve further into such a shallow, inconsequential world. There are thick Russian novels of consequence, thrilling detective yarns, slim volumes of verse, and fat tomes of fact, all beckoning from the shelves of your local bookstore. There are memoirs of people who suffered terrible diseases or grew up in Ireland, biographies of great and noble celebrities, and how-to books on every subject under the sun. Is Harris, who does *nothing*, so worthy of your attention?

The answer must be a resounding *yes*, for to understand humanity one must look not only at the prominent few marching down the center street of life's parade, nor just the many watching from the sidelines, but also those who overslept and missed the whole procession. Kings and slaves, labor and capital, mermaids and pirates, of these the world has heard plenty. Yet that man sitting in a dark bar on a weeknight, complaining about the music and undertipping as he buys his third martini—he has flown under the radar.

We cannot guess how many of these oversleepers there are for they are always at the liquor store when the census taker calls. Yet the spirit of philosophical inquiry demands we examine them, if only to discover how it is they manage to have no effect on anything whatsoever. Even drug addicts, hobos, and sexual deviates register on the historical record through statistics and crime reports, yet Harris could disappear tomorrow (or for that matter, duplicate himself a thousand times over) and have less effect on the future than the death of a butterfly that has never flapped its wings. This, I contend, is an achievement in and of itself, richly deserving of after-school specials, trenchant editorials in the *Times*, and (I hope) this book.

CHAPTER 7

SHOPPING

Harris awoke on Saturday afternoon feeling, instead of his customary gloom, a strange mixture of exuberance and agitation. His usually dormant libido had been subtly inflamed by the thought of relocating from Maxine's apartment, a shrine to femininity, littered with glamour magazines, styling products, frocks, and wigs, to a messy flat with a bunch of guys. Being both above and averse to anything so base as animal passions, however, Harris failed to recognize his friskiness for what it was and decided he was likely suffering from a new and potentially fatal disease. He lay perfectly still for twenty minutes waiting for more symptoms to develop. When they did not, he finally roused himself for another day.

But not all was as it had been. Things were somehow . . . better. A stranger could be forgiven for failing to notice the change, but someone intimately familiar with Harris, some professor of Harrisology, would have observed an unusual dearth of regretful sighs and exasperated moans as he heaved himself out of bed. They would have seen his posture, normally curved like a candy cane, unfurl to nearly straight, adding inches to his height and a dollop of dignity to his carriage. And if they could've eavesdropped on his thoughts, they would have noticed his ceaseless lamentations were inflected with a hint of irony. That the universe was rigged against him seemed more of an occasion for amused cynicism than bitter self-pity.

Though perpetually destitute, Harris went shopping every Saturday and so, in a buoyant mood, he set off for Hayes Valley. Strolling through the newly gentrified neighborhood's streets, he imagined himself at one with the urban sophisticates around him, people who regularly vacationed abroad, visited art museums, and prepared clever meals using sleek, modern cooking utensils. So intoxicating was this dream of tasteful prosperity that he indulged himself by purchasing a tube of apricot-kelp replenishing derma-scrub with micro-granules that he really couldn't afford. Alas, only a few moments after said purchase, Harris's mood plummeted when he passed by a shop whimsically named, Somewhat Appealing Clothes. The large front window featured a bald female mannequin wearing an exquisitely beautiful dress of gray and lavender tulle shredded and sewn together so as to look like a massive cloud of feathers. Clever, lovely, and daringly original, the sight made Harris first gasp, then keen inwardly. *I will never be a fashion designer!*

You see, as a youth Harris had cherished hopes of becoming a couturier. He drew innumerable sketches of extremely thin, tall women wearing flamboyant outfits and blasé expressions that he taped to the walls of his bedroom. When questioned by his worried parents about these he spoke lovingly of Balenciaga, Schiaparelli, and Coco Chanel, the names sliding off his tongue like the sheerest poetry. (Adventurous readers may wish to try this at home. *Bal-en'-see-aaah'-gah. Skeeey-ap-ar-el-ee.* Fun, isn't it?) Upon graduating high school and moving to San Francisco, Harris began frequenting North Beach cafes where he loitered elegantly and alcoholically, rehearsing for a future that surely would include significant leisure time in Paris and Milan. He even took to wearing a black suit jacket draped over his shoulders as if it were a short cape.

It was quite a blow, then, when his application to fashion school was rejected. Harris then fell back on Plan B: indifferently laboring at a string of dead-end jobs while wallowing in a toxic morass of petulance and self-pity. He liked, when drinking brown liquor and feeling moody, to say this was due to his "chronic depression." As in, "It may not be *entirely* your fault that I'm such a failure, Mother, but *you do realize* that you must have passed on a gene for chronic depression?" Or, "I can't pay you back that ninety-two dollars I owe you. My chronic depression has made working utterly impossible this week." Since Harris shunned psychology, psychiatry, and counseling of any kind ("Thanks for implying I'm mentally ill, that *really* makes me feel good!" he would spit accusingly at anyone suggesting such a thing) it is something of a mystery how he came upon this diagnosis.

As Harris stood gazing at the store window in a state of emotional semi-devastation, a busty young woman wearing a colorful '60s paisley party frock ran up to him. "Harris!" she squealed. Harris recognized her as a friend of friends and tried to recall her name, but was momentarily flummoxed. In small cities one runs into everyone in one's extended circle (friends of friends, roommates of friends, co-workers of roommates, lovers of co-workers, and such like combinations) often enough that remembering names is easy and therefore expected. In large cities, remembering everyone's name would be utterly impossible, and is therefore not expected. In medium-sized San Francisco, remembering everyone's name is sort of possible and therefore sort-of expected, an impossibly awkward situation that aggravates the social anxiety of people far less neurotic than Harris.

In this instance, however, Harris was aided in his mnemonic quest by a strong component of desire. Not for the woman-in-question's body (heaven forbid!), but the rather the expensive camera slung around her neck. Harris loved having his picture taken. The relevant information surfaced in his consciousness. Name: Vivian. Type: bisexual stripper (though not all pious and political about it). Status: popular, probably due to her willingness to take pictures of social-climbing narcissists for little or no money.

"Harris, sweetie, good to see you!" trilled Vivian.

"Hi Vivian. I see you have your camera with you."

"Yeah, I just came from a shoot with Sir Benedict, you know, the club columnist? He's so funny. He dressed up like Little Debbie, you know, from Little Debbie Snack Cakes?"

"What was this for?"

"He needed a new headshot for his website."

Harris shook his head mournfully. "So he's jumped on the internet bandwagon too."

"He still has his column in the paper."

"A column that never seems to mention my name, not that I care."

"Well, he has to cover a lot of ground," said Vivian. She glanced at her watch in a manner Harris found rather artificial. "Well, I should be going. Nice seeing you!"

Harris, eyes locked on the camera, issued a short plea. "Wait!" His mind rummaged about for a follow up. "Looks like I'm going to be moving into Wally's place."

Vivian's eyebrows shot upward. "I *love* Wally! Have you seen *Dawn: Portrait of A Teenage Runaway* yet?"

Harris put on a thoughtful look. "No, actually. I like Wally, but his plays are—and I admit this is based on hearsay because I haven't actually seen any—a bit *corny*."

"It's hilarious," said Vivian. "And Wally is so nice! He let me run off flyers for my last opening for *free* at the copy shop where he works. People should be nicer to Wally. He's a real asset to the queer arts community."

"What I'm wondering is if maybe Wally's plays aren't maybe, you know, formulaic."

Vivian waxed rhapsodic. "They have these *incredible* polyester outfits, and the dances are *perfectly* synchronized."

Harris spoke over Vivian's testimonial. "Or maybe formulaic isn't the right word. Maybe hackneyed. Or maybe I mean trite. You know, Camp 101 for straight people."

"Listen, sweetie," Vivian backed away as she spoke, "I would *love* to talk more but I *cannot* be late. I'll see you around, Okay? Ciao." Vivian sprinted off.

"Okay, later," said Harris, wearing a perturbed face meant to imply that Vivian was rudely deserting him.

By the time he arrived back at his apartment, or rather *Maxine's* apartment, Harris's mood had swung back from dampened to frisky. Luckily, Maxine was out so he had the bathroom all to himself and was able to spend twenty minutes cleansing his face with the micro-granules, his hands using small, circular motions as prescribed by the product's detailed instructions, which he read in full despite the tiny print. Rinsing off, Harris decided that yes, he did look better, perhaps even *younger.* It was this unusually happy thought that danced around his brain as he lay down for a disco nap, for once not taking the time to curse cruel fate for forcing him to sleep on such a miserable, lumpy, and thoroughly substandard sofa-bed.

CHAPTER 8

A SICK PAL

"HEY BEAUTIFUL!" CALLED OUT A MIDDLE-AGED African American man peddling clothes and sundries against a fence surrounding a parking lot. *The nerve!* thought Maxine, quickening her pace. Men often flung demeaning epithets or sexually aggressive remarks her way; in response she tried to project an air of untouchable classiness, floating along city streets with the exaggerated poise and hauteur of a debutante in a twenty-thousand-dollar ball gown.

The man tried again. "I got some choice items for sale here. Bargain prices."

Maxine, who loved bargains, stopped to glance at the man's wares. Spread out on a blanket at his feet were a few disco records, some hardcover Steven King novels, a box of People magazines, and a few children's dolls in various states of decomposition. Then she saw, hung on the fence with a wire hanger, a *to-die-for* '60s-style white vinyl trench coat.

"Name's Ralph," said the man holding out his hand. Maxine loathed hard sales pitches, but Ralph's gray hair, affable smile, and pleasingly relaxed demeanor disarmed her. "Maxine," she said, not taking his hand but offering a little wave instead. "Maxine Du Maurier."

"Pretty name for a pretty lady," said Ralph. He gestured at his merchandise. "Take a look. Rock bottom prices. Priced to move, as we say in the business."

Hoping to pay as little as possible, Maxine tried to sound blasé as she asked, "Might I try on that coat?"

The man took it off the fence and handed it to her. "A real fine coat. And for you . . ." Ralph looked Maxine up and down appraisingly. "Twelve dollars."

Maxine put on the coat. It was a little too large, but only a little, and she immediately loved it with all her heart. "I thought you were going to give me a *bargain*," she purred flirtatiously.

Ralph smiled. "Gotta run my business, don't I? Problem is these days not enough people mind their own business 'cause not enough people got a business to mind. Everybody needs a calling. Me, I'm a salesman."

"I'm a chanteuse," said Maxine smiling prettily and walking over to admire her reflection in the plate glass window of a store next to the fence.

"Is that right?" Ralph emitted an artificially good-natured chuckle. "Now I thought you might be in show business. I saw you coming down the street in that fancy outfit like something out of some ol' movie, and I said to myself, as I live and breathe, that woman has *got* to be in show business!"

"It's kind of like a spy coat," Maxine observed. "Oh, I simply must have it! Unfortunately, I'm a little short of cash, *but* I've got some tickets to my next show at Big Louie's. They're worth ten dollars each. I'll trade you two for this coat. You'll be ahead eight bucks." She began searching through her purse. "Now where can they be?"

Ralph waved his hands frantically. "No, no. I don't make no deals like that. Not for such a fine coat. How about ten dollars?"

Maxine sighed and counted out her cash. "I'll give you my last seven bucks and here we go, one ticket to my show. You'll absolutely love it, I do "Downtown," the Petula Clark song?"

"I always liked that song," said Ralph. He pondered a moment. "Oh, all right, just this once on account of I like to help out a pretty lady in show business." He smoothed the crumpled bills Maxine handed him along with the crumpled ticket to her gig and stuffed them in his wallet. "Yessiree," he agreed once he'd looked up to see Maxine still examining herself in the flattering reflection. "It do indeed make you look something like a secret agent."

"White is definitely my color. I don't know how to thank you." Maxine imagined herself in the coat singing "Diamonds Are Forever," or better yet, "You Only Live Twice."

"Pleasure's all mine," said Ralph, already looking around for his next customer.

"Ciao," said Maxine. She began striding up the street with new clothing confidence. A couple of blocks later she arrived at her destination: the hospice where Oliver, her old pal from the Summer Campers, was living. As she opened the door, a crazy quilt of emotions came over her. Sadness (naturally) for her friend's pitiful condition, but also fear brought about by proximity to disease, excitement occasioned by the situation's life and death drama, guilt at enjoying that excitement (just a little bit), and pride in her moral scrupulousness at feeling that guilt. Squelching all of that, she announced herself to the receptionist. "Here to see Oliver Oberstein."

As she spoke, Oliver, wearing a lemon chiffon frock that would have made him look like one of the Supremes had he not been an anemically thin white man in early middle-age with two day's beard growth, wheeled into the hallway crooning, "Come live with me, and be my love, if only for a daaaay. Come live with me and see my love, how fast it fades, awaaaay. . ."

"You never could sing," said Maxine.

"Is that any way to talk about a dying woman?" barked Oliver. "Wheel me to my room. It's freezing in here." Maxine took hold of the chair and pushed Oliver down the hallway from which he'd made his entrance. "That door on the left," said Oliver, pointing. "Which you'd know if you'd ever visited."

"One gets so terribly busy," said Maxine in the breathy voice of a spoiled debutante. "Shopping, fittings, balls. . ."

The joke made itself, but Oliver voiced it anyway. "Busy with *balls*, yes, I can imagine." As they entered Oliver's room, Maxine's head reeled from the odor of gardenia perfume mixed with the sour smell of illness. She parked his wheelchair and sat on his bed. "You just might be interested in this," said Oliver in a casual voice as he pulled a thin paperback off the dresser and handed it to Maxine.

Maxine squinted as she examined the book. "Wow! I thought it came out on the first."

"That's the release party," said Oliver.

Maxine read aloud from the back cover. "With his literary debut, *Dougie Doodles and the Enchanted Gay Bar: Sad and Meaningless Fables for an Imploding Society,* Oliver J. Oberstein intermarries morbid humor and a keen eye for social detail to produce a series of dyspeptic fairytales for modern nihilists."

"That, my dear, is your very own personal copy. Hang on to it. It's an autographed first edition and will no doubt be extremely valuable some day."

"Thanks." Maxine shoved the book into her purse.

"Ah, the life of a literati," said Oliver. "I shall have to invite Truman, Gore, and Tennessee to my next cocktail party."

"I'm kicking Harris out of my apartment," said Maxine.

Oliver's eyebrows raised in delighted expectation. "Do tell!"

Recounting the particulars of the fight suddenly seemed like too much trouble to Maxine. "Oh, I just got tired of him."

Oliver smiled evilly. "Well, good riddance to bad rubbish."

"What's your beef with Harris?" asked Maxine.

Oliver leaned forward and spoke in the low voice he reserved for juicy gossip. "Once I mentioned to him I was featuring at an open mic and he immediately said, in this jaded Eurotrash party princess voice, 'How *tired*.' That drunken little worm has never even *been* to an open mic, so how would he know? And need I point out, that there is nothing in the universe more tired than calling something tired?"

As omniscient narrator I feel obliged to mention that Harris had in fact been to an open mic once, albeit accidentally. He and Wally had been getting soused in a bar when two-dozen sober-looking people came in radiating anxiety and ambition. One by one, they sat themselves around a low wooden stage, feverishly muttering and jotting in notebooks. Wally and Harris paid this invasion no mind until a shabbily dressed fellow took the stage, produced a microphone, and delivered a hectoring speech about the importance of poetry followed by an admonition not to read for more than five minutes. Feeling intruded upon, Wally and Harris continued their conversation, raising their voices slightly to be heard over the amplified readers.

First up was a man with a graying ponytail who launched into what sounded like an editorial from *The Nation* lambasting American imperialism, which he nonetheless read in syncopated meter as if it were a poem. Harris and Wally glared at him as if he were defecating in public, but to no effect. The man droned on well past the five-minute limit, but the M.C., in solidarity with the man's political sentiments, allowed him to continue. Next, a beefy guy performed a self-pitying and slightly scatological comedy routine, after which a young man read a first-person piece about his depraved alcoholism, which was followed by a long meditation from a middle-aged woman about her breakfast and the importance of compassion, followed by another young man's harrowing tale of child abuse. When a kinkily dressed woman began reciting an ode to her girlfriend's genitalia in an oddly braying voice, Wally and Harris conceded defeat and slunk out. It was of this dispiriting event that Harris thought when he spat out "How *tired*" to Oliver.

"So who's gonna be your new roomie?"

"I only threw him out yesterday, so I haven't found anyone yet. I don't *really* need to rush as I've got my gig at Big Louie's on Monday. Last month I made almost two hundred dollars!"

"I'd move in myself if I weren't dying. Won't be long now. Sweet Chariot gonna be swingin' low, comin' for to carry me home. Yesiree, woman, I'll be six feet under by Christmas." He cackled.

Maxine felt irritated. "Quit with the dramatics. Nobody's dying of AIDS anymore. It's become quite passé. Simply isn't done."

Oliver ignored this. "Hey, did you see my author photo? Look at my author photo!"

Maxine dug the book out of her purse and turned to the last page. There she saw a photo of a pleasantly plump Oliver standing at a bus stop wearing an infinitely weary look and a conservative tweed skirt suit while holding a parasol with one hand and a nude boy on a leash with the other. "Awww, from the Summer Campers last show," said Maxine, plunging the book back into her purse. She looked up. "You know sweetie, you've lost *a lot* of weight. Have you been eating your suppers like a good girl?"

"For the first time in my life I'm supermodel thin, and you want me to *gain* weight?"

"Just a little," said Maxine. "And by the way, look at my new secret agent coat!" She stood and modeled.

"Divine," said Oliver, without enthusiasm.

The pair prattled on, reminiscing—the time a fan on God-only-knows-what-drugs rushed the stage and popped Franny's water balloon breasts with a hatpin! The time Brandy Whine's lesbian sister from U. Mass visited the Summer Campers's flat and tried to raise everybody's consciousness!—and dishing for another half-hour: "Princess Pam's cherry red hair dye made her look cheap!" "Lolly finally went and married that creepy bass player?" Then Oliver stifled a yawn.

"You know Maxi, thanks for coming and all, but I think I need a nap. Dying really takes it out of me."

"Puhleaze," snapped Maxine, sincerely irritated by her friend's morbidity. "You're *not* dying."

Oliver smiled slyly. "Well, not before my book release party, anyway,"

CHAPTER 9

"DOUGIE DOODLES AND THE ENCHANTED GAY BAR" BY OLIVER J. OBERSTEIN

ONCE UPON A TIME IN A foggy, faraway kingdom, there was an enchanted gay bar where none of the patrons ever said anything sensible, wore anything decent, or went home alone. Legend had it that a powerful witch by the name of Janis Joplin had once gone drinking there and, charmed by a patron's joie de vivre, serenaded them with a magic song. Ever since, it had been the loudest, crudest, darkest, strangest, and all around most alarming nightspot in all the land. Despite (or perhaps because of) these qualities, it was heaps more fun than any of the nice bars where nobody got twizzled in the coat-check room or committed acts of unspeakable depravity behind the ice machine.

One day, a cabal of repressed, self-loathing wizards from one of the more tedious local taverns got into a jealous snit and cast an evil curse on the enchanted gay bar: half the patrons were doomed to die horribly before the next Oscars, a few months hence. When the bar's patrons received the wizards's bitchy letter informing them of the curse, they pretended not to care. "So we'll die young," they said, with insouciant flips of their youthful locks. "So what? Who wants to be a wrinkle queen anyway?"

This pretense of courage continued even after a popular rent boy froze to death while playing Ms. Pacman, permafrost covering his skin with a whitish sheen and tiny icicles dangling from his ears and nose. A week later, a few people admitted to some slight dismay when a disco queen imploded on the dance floor, his body shriveling up like fruit left in the sun till there was nothing left but sequins, dust, and the faint smell of poppers. When next a slumming billionaire burst into flames whilst trying to seduce a gorgeous go-go dancer, the bar descended into a barely subdued panic.

Some regulars began staying home, hoping the curse wouldn't affect them so long as they remained in their hovels watching videos and eating pizza. "Call us as soon as it's all over!" they suggested with bright, nervous smiles. Others, more favorably disposed to drama, refused to leave the bar for any reason and had to live on cocktail olives and complimentary peanuts. "We don't want to miss a single minute of this," they enthused. Still others came and went as usual but ratcheted up the level of frenzy by a notch or six. Competitive perversion, hysterical glibness, and quasi-religious ecstasy (as well as the other kind) became epidemic. Some wags claimed the bar was even more fun than it had been before the nasty old curse.

Into this ghastly scene walked a young lad by the name of Dougie Doodles. Like most of the bar's patrons, he came from a godforsaken Hellhole on the wrong side of the rainbow and was only too glad to find a place where nobody expected much of him beyond looking wicked cute.

"Hey, what's up?" asked Dougie of no one in particular.

A regular by the name of Edwin, dashingly dressed in a blue blazer with an impeccably folded cravat, turned to Dougie and explained, "A cabal of evil wizards, jealous of our joie de vivre, has cursed this, our enchanted gay bar, and we're dropping off like teenagers in a *Friday the Thirteenth* sequel. Many have fled in horror, but those of us who remain find our fears mounting ominously, for no one has yet discovered a way to halt the specter of death that stalks us as the lions of the Serengeti stalk the wild gazelles."

"Will you buy me a drink?" asked Dougie with a winsome smile.

"Surely, my dear boy!" said Edwin, who knew full well that in buying a drink, one buys an audience. He purchased the boy a Singapore Sling and began a longwinded monologue on the perils of sunshine, waterbeds, and reggae music. As the night wore on, Edwin bought for Dougie a Sex on the Beach, then a Kamikaze, after which a Long Island Iced Tea, and finally a Blue Moon.

Wowee zowee! thought Dougie as he drank and drank, *This Edwin character doesn't seem half-bad for a decrepit old geezer. Truly, this enchanted gay bar is an awesome place for an underappreciated youth like myself, in spite of the terrible curse. I mean, what with all these complimentary cocktails and all.*

Simultaneously Edwin thought, *Surely this enchanted gay bar is still a blissful haven in life's sea of sorrows despite the unnaturally high mortality rate, for here one can still ensnare a boy comely enough to be used in television advertisements for deep fried potato snacks or toothpaste with the simple outlay of sixty-two dollars worth of liquor.*

That night Dougie went home to Edwin's microscopic apartment and never left except to accompany his new benefactor to the enchanted bar each evening. While other regulars slurred their words, danced the hoochie coochie, and thought nothing of crawling around on all fours if the spirit (or spirits) so moved them, Edwin spent each night sitting primly on his barstool imbibing liqueurs and spouting witty, bitter epigrams. *What a perfect gentleman my Edwin is,* thought Dougie.

Over the next few weeks, Dougie noticed that the regulars were given to surreptitiously making goo-goo eyes at him. Whenever this happened, he stared at the floor to hide his blushing boyish face. Edwin tried to ignore this until one night, as he was railing against fake wood paneling, home mortgage deductions, and roast beef, he snapped, "Dear boy, I know being the youngest and prettiest thing in a bar where youth and beauty are valued beyond emeralds and rubies must be terribly diverting, but would you be so good as to pay attention to me while I'm expostulating?" Before Dougie could respond, a nearby hoochie coochie dancer exploded, splattering sticky, bloody, gooey body parts all over them. "Eeek!" shrieked Edwin, fainting off his barstool.

Jeez, shrieking eek's not a very dudely reaction, thought Dougie disapprovingly. While the bartender tried to revive Edwin with brandy and cocaine, Dougie went to the bathroom to wash off the gore. There he discovered a Viking, fully six-foot-three, with long, braided, blond hair and icy blue eyes.

"Let me help you clean up," said the Viking, who proceeded to whip off the boy's clothes and ravish him with kisses. Before Dougie could have said his name, he found himself in a nearby alley engaged in an act explicitly forbidden by the Book of Leviticus. The great hulking Norseman seemed to know secrets about Dougie's body of which Dougie himself was unaware, and the boy convulsed with pleasure. When at last the carnal delirium subsided, Dougie said, "Wowee zowee, that was fun! What was that?" (For you see, Edwin had always been too glamorously repressed to touch Dougie, and the boy was a virgin.)

"That was sex," said the Viking as he zipped up his trousers. "That's the reason most everyone comes here night after night instead of working proper jobs or raising families."

"I love you," said Dougie.

And with that, the Viking melted. Not melted as in falling in love with Dougie in return, but literally due to the annoying curse.

Yikes! thought Dougie, *this place is giving me the heebie-jeebies. I'm gonna find me a bar where everyone isn't always melting and blowing up and imploding and stuff.* And so, without even bidding Edwin good-bye, Dougie wandered off into the fog. For forty days and forty nights he went from bar to bar, looking for one that suited his fancy. Alas, each and every one of the unenchanted bars lacked zest. And if there was anything more depressing than zestlessness, Dougie sure didn't know what it was.

Finally, in desperation, Dougie headed for Sleaze Street where zest was reputedly plentiful. There, amidst pool halls, whiskey bars, pawnshops, and some really quite excellent and reasonably priced Vietnamese restaurants, he discovered a gaggle of wayward waifs. A few sat huddled on the hard, cement sidewalks morosely smoking cigarettes and cursing fate. Others perched in trees hooting like chimpanzees, their eyes as wild as madmen's. Still others, alone and mysterious, darted betwixt cars and shadows. *I guess this is sort of zesty,* thought Dougie.

Almost immediately a handsome moppet, albeit one possessed of a stare vacant enough to frighten tourists, spied Dougie and skateboarded over. "I'm Hector," he said.

"I'm Dougie," replied Dougie. Without another word, the boys fell into a dumpster and made love with furious abandon. Once finished, they clambered out onto the sidewalk, tucking in their shirts, running their fingers through their hair, and smiling sheepishly.

"So, whadaya wanna do now?" asked Dougie.

"I dunno, what do you wanna do?" asked Hector.

"I dunno," said Dougie. The pair lapsed into a deafening silence.

"What you children need," said an enterprising salesman, on surveying their lethargic forms slumped in the gutter, "is some oblivion."

"Sure, whatever," Hector and Dougie said, hardly bothering to glance up.

The reader of these pages scarcely needs be told the oblivion provided was deceptively affordable, but that the boys loved it and were quickly enslaved by their need for more, available only at a premium price. The pair (as is customary in such situations) took up residence in a fleabag hotel and began fleecing geezers at nearby watering holes to pay for their ruinously expensive habit. Hector resented the work.

"All this hustling seriously cuts into my TV time," he groused. "If it weren't for the thrill of *schtupping* my darling Dougie, I'd skeedadle."

Dougie, on the other hand, was content. "This is livin'!" he crowed often and loudly.

It seemed a lifetime, yet it was only a few months, before oblivion use ravaged the boys's exquisite looks. They went from handsome to average to interesting to not-so-very-interesting. Scrounging money for oblivion became near impossible. "This is no fun anymore," said Hector. "I'm going to community college to learn the skills I need to become a professional systems analyst. Ciao, Dougie."

Dougie bewailed his fate. "All I wanted was non-stop sensual delight with no accompanying risk or effort, and now I'm stranded in a substandard hotel room with nothing to eat but Top Ramen and a television that doesn't even get channel two. This is total bunk!" Then he chanced to recall his former life with Edwin. *That was sort of okay,* he thought, and he ran as fast as his enfeebled legs would carry him back to the enchanted gay bar.

As it was the day before the Oscars, Dougie found the place considerably thinned out. The few remaining patrons were histrionically depressed, all except Edwin, who sat on his old stool holding forth on the evils of white chocolate, secretarial work, and temperance. On seeing Dougie, he interrupted his disquisition to murmur, "Dear Dougie, is that you?" Dougie nodded and Edwin cried out, "First you disappear without warning, then you return *without* your astounding good looks. Whatever is the meaning of this?"

"Well, I learned a valuable lesson . . ." began Dougie. Before he could finish his sentence, however, the dreadful curse hit. Dougie's body transmogrified into a cloud of pink cotton candy, and he was dead.

CHAPTER 10

SATURDAY NIGHT ON THE TOWN

HARRIS WOKE FROM HIS DISCO NAP when the vulgarians in the apartment next door began blasting druggy, discordant rap at top volume. Still tired, he reluctantly rose and put a CD on his boombox to drown it out. The admixture of Roxy Music and the idiotically chanted chorus from next door—"Insane in the membrane! Insane in the membrane!"—would have been unendurable without anaesthetization, which Harris prudently kept at hand in the form of a bottle of vodka hidden (safe from Maxine's voracious thirst) under his sofa. A few swigs later, an emboldened Harris banged on the wall adjoining the offending apartment with the flat of his hand. "Turn it down," he shrieked in a firm voice. Miraculously, the volume lowered slightly. Flushed with victory, Harris began dressing for the evening's revelry.

Still enflamed by spring fever, Harris chose an unusually provocative ensemble: tight, low-waist blue jeans; punky-junkie black boots; and best of all, a vintage sleeveless t-shirt emblazoned with the image of an old hillbilly woman smoking a pipe on the porch of a comically run-down shack and the slogan "Ain't No Place Like Home" written in a faux-rustic typeface composed of twigs. *I look positively do-able,* he thought as he ambled down to the Stud.

It was a boisterous night. Everyone complained cheerily about the lack of space and air as they pressed themselves into the throng. Harris slithered through the crowd to his favorite spot at the end of the bar and, after a long wait for the busy bartender, ordered a Whiskey Sour, a concoction he loathed and would therefore drink slowly instead of chug-a-lugging as he would something tasty like a Cosmopolitan. All around, a swirl of twenty-somethings exhibited the glee and zest their age group is so justifiably renowned for. And these weren't just any youngsters. These were design students, photoshoot assistants, and kids who worked at vintage clothing boutiques, people of *taste* and *style.* Hands were raised in the air like they just didn't care, hips slipped, hair flipped, and feet got movin' to the dancin' beat. Oh, it was a party! First witty banter, then flirtation, and finally sexual groping made their appearances as Harris watched, waiting for something to draw him into the vortex of fun. It was near midnight when that something arrived in the form of Lance. A wee bit portly with rosy cheeks and twinkling eyes, Lance's physiognomy suggested jollity, but due to his sour disposition friends most frequently described him as a useless, bitter old queen.

"Tick, tick, tick," said Lance, surprising Harris from behind. Ever since Harris had imprudently mentioned a few weeks earlier that he dreaded his impending fortieth birthday, Lance had greeted him in this cruel, clocklike manner.

"Could that be Lance Fantastic?" asked Harris turning around and feigning delight.

Lance (née Lance Butterfield) winced. When he'd first arrived in S.F. he'd called himself Lance Fantastic and claimed to be the twin of another handsome barfly he'd vaguely resembled known as Wesley Wonder. A three-way with "The Twins" was considered a sexual delicacy and rite of passage for bar regulars. Their reign of sexual supremacy ended when, without warning, Quaaludes, their favorite intoxicant, went off the market. Feeling the deprivation keenly, the pair turned to distilled spirits for comfort. Unfortunately, as their drinking got heavier, so did they. Worse luck, this occurred just as the first blush of youth faded from their cheeks. The twin act, once seen as a charmingly youthful affectation, began to strike people as creepy. The boys split up and everyone quit using their assumed surnames—except Harris when he was being hateful.

"Good evening Harris, you miserable old cow," said Lance.

Harris's face remained placid. "Lance, your once lively wit has been replaced with something that resembles wit, but is actually cold, hard, and dead like stone. Scientifically speaking, I would say your wit has petrified."

"Quit this bitchery and give Mommy a hug!" Lance leaned toward Harris as if to embrace him. Though Lance had stopped several inches short of physical contact, Harris shrunk back like a slug covered in salt.

"Cut it out!"

Lance, withdrew.

"God," said Harris. "The crowd tonight . . . I don't know who all these people are, and I don't think I want to."

Lance snorted. "Listen Granny, ten years ago all the old queens were saying the same thing about you."

Harris's voice took on an aggrieved tone. "Please! Everything about this new generation is tired. It's an objective fact. They're probably all going home later to their Pottery Barn furnished apartments so they can felch each other while listening to house music."

"Oh, whatever," said Lance.

"Kindly refrain from using that word in my presence," said Harris. "Or else."

Lance stood on his tiptoes and glanced around. "You haven't seen Jack-O-Lantern, have you?" he asked, referring to a friend whose smile was conspicuously short on teeth. "If I don't get a little something I'm liable to get depressed."

"What possible reason could you have for being depressed?" asked Harris, with a sickly grin. "Here we are in this fabulous nightclub full of delectable disco dollies, and they're playing all this fabulous music, and serving up fabulous drinks, and we're all fabulous. Just snap out of it, Myrtle!"

Lance winced. "Can it, Hildegard. I need coke."

"Well, now that you mention it," said Harris, "I might want to go in on a little something."

"Upfront," said Lance, his light blue eyes fixing Harris with a steely glare.

Harris wiggled his mustache as he searched for plausible explanations as to why he should be extended credit but found none. He stealthily dug a few bills out of his wallet and tucked them into Lance's hand.

"Right back," said Lance, disappearing with business-like haste into the crowd.

Harris leaned against the wall and surveyed the bar just as the collective vibe of sexy hilarity became so overwhelming that everyone forgot all about the impending ecological apocalypse and their stupid jobs. It became the sort of night that purveyors of beer would sell their souls to incorporate into TV commercials. There was not an inch of spare space, yet more and more people were pushing in, desperate to be part of what was turning into a legendary evening.

"Bad news," said Lance when he finally returned.

"Can't find Jack?" asked Harris.

"He's dead," said Lance.

Harris paused while his brain tried to reorganize itself. "Uh," he said finally, "you're saying he died?

Lance frowned. "That's what my sources tell me."

Harris's face assumed a skeptical cast. "Are you sure? I mean, couldn't this be a rumor?"

"Happened the day before yesterday. Heart attack. Right over there in front of the deejay booth." Lance heaved a sigh. "Everyone just went right on dancing."

Harris's mind whirled. "Jeez. Dead. I wonder . . . was it like an overdose or was he was dancing too hard? I mean, of course he was a little older than us, in his forties for sure, maybe even early fifties, and doing cocaine all the time, which is totally not healthy. And we really shouldn't be doing it either. It's probably a blessing we can't now. You have to treat your body like a temple, not a trash can. Cocaine? You might as well eat bacon grease sandwiches for breakfast, lunch, and dinner. Not that I'm saying Jack ate that way, I really don't know what he ate. And maybe it was the opposite. Maybe he didn't eat enough. He could have had malnutrition from only doing cocaine and not eating. I only very rarely eat red meat, so I don't think that I *personally* would be likely to have a heart attack. Especially now that I don't really drink any more. I mean, yes, I'm drinking tonight, but I don't go out every night of the week like Jack might have and maybe he had a few cocktails at every place he went to and maybe that was a contributing factor to his heart attack, which might have been from some genetic defect that had nothing to do with drugs or diet or drinking or dancing. And I don't have a family history of heart disease, except my dad's sister, who had a murmur. So yeah, it's really sad about Jack, though I guess maybe out of respect we shouldn't call him that anymore. Do you remember what his real name was?"

"You're detestable," said Lance.

Harris's back stiffened and his tone sharpened. "Because I don't remember some *drug dealer's* name? I barely knew him!"

Lance groaned. "God, it's scary how many people we know have died. Our peer group is disappearing."

"We should just call them our disa*peer* group," suggested Harris.

"I guess they haven't *all* died," said Lance. "Lots moved away. Or got jobs. Real ones that make you get up in the morning."

"Cut the crap, Mabel, most of our pals are pushin' up daisies."

Lance had a retort, and Harris a retort for that, but out of humanitarian concern I will spare the reader a blow-by-blow accounting of the next ninety minutes during which Harris and Lance assaulted each other with dispiriting observations and withering remarks and pick up our story shortly after last call when the hunky bartender bellowed out, "You don't have to go home, but you can't stay here!" As the bar disgorged its tipsified patrons, Harris flowed with the crowd onto the street. Once there, he heard the shrill-yet-still-somehow-tinkle-y voice of his diminutive pal, Sasa Bacabuhay, successful hairdresser and queen-about-town.

"Herb, where are you going? You'll miss the sidewalk sale!" Harris caught sight of Sasa, dressed in flawlessly chic-yet-casual Italian designer wear, standing at the curb.

"Sidewalk sale?" asked Herb, a cute, gangly, redhead who'd been walking off alone, his hands thrust into the pockets of a fancy silver parka.

"Oh, you are precious, Herb!" announced Sasa for all to hear. "A sidewalk sale is what we sophisticated urban homosexuals call cruising the sidewalk in front of a bar that's closing." He walked up to Herb and began massaging the lad's shoulders, no easy task as he was five-foot-three to Herb's six-foot-two. "Poor Herb. Stranded all those years in Idaho amongst the straight people."

"Sure is cold out," observed Herb as he wriggled free from Sasa.

"True," admitted Sasa. "All right, let's go home." He faced the diehards milling about in front of the bar and called out in a sarcastically perky voice, "Anyone up for drinks *chez moi?*"

CHAPTER 11

SUBURBAN SOJOURN

The Black Rose, Maxine's favorite bar, was crowded with men. She hadn't so much as had to drop a hankie before one of them bought her a drink and made an indecent proposal. Rudy was bald, bulky in that over-done bodybuilder way she loved, and (best of all) stood a mere five-foot-five, only a few inches taller than she. Maxine enjoyed being the smaller half of a couple, but not *too* much smaller. Rudy drove her to his apartment, some-where in the hinterlands of the East Bay, where they spent three-quarters of an hour making whoopee. Once their passion was fully spent, Maxine sat up and switched on a bedside lamp. "God, Rudy, you were fantastic," she cooed. "Got any beer?"

Rudy shook his head. "Nah, too many carbs."

Maxine waited a beat then said in her best "fun" voice, "I know, let s go out for drinks!"

"Nah," said Rudy. "Nowhere to go."

Maxine imitated a spoiled chorus girl she'd once seen in an old B movie. "Aw, ya big galoot, ya never take me anywheres!" Rudy, having never seen a chorus girl in an old B movie, was confused and said nothing. A change of tactics was in order. "C'mon, Rudy. I wanna show you off to all the other gals, make 'em drool with jealousy."

Rudy lifted himself out of bed. "All right, if it'll make you happy. Just for a little while." He dropped to the floor and began doing push-ups.

"A few drinks, a few dances, and few laughs, and then we come back here and screw our brains out some more," said Maxine.

Rudy sat on the edge of the bed and made dissatisfied faces as he felt his biceps. He reminded Maxine of a huge, muscular potato. Hot! She grabbed her things and went into the bathroom to put herself together. After turning on the faucet on to mask suspicious noises she opened the medicine cabinet and rooted around. Amidst the over-the-counter cold remedies was a bottle of Xanax. Maxine popped two, downing them with tap water.

Back in the bedroom, Maxine found Rudy wearing skin-tight stonewash jeans, puffy white tennis shoes, and a tank top with a neckline so low his pectoral muscles looked as if they might pop out at any second. "Can we go back to the Black Rose?" she asked.

Rudy shook his head. "Nah, too far. It's already kinda late." He paused for a moment, no doubt racking his brain for a local watering hole where he wouldn't mind being seen with Maxine. "There's the White Horse over in Oakland, but if any of those fags make a pass at me, we're leaving."

"Anyone makes a pass at you, man, woman, child, animal, vegetable, or mineral, and I'll claw their eyes, out." Maxine made a little clawing motion with her hand.

"Vegetables and minerals don't have eyes," objected Rudy.

"Potatoes do," countered Maxine. Rudy laughed like that was a good joke.

On arriving at the bar, Rudy and Maxine discovered the place was hosting its weekly amateur drag show/lip-synch contest. Maxine felt relieved they'd have something to talk about. She'd learned on the way over that Rudy was no prize conversationalist. On the tiny stage a big boned gal was sassing her way through the old '80s hit "Destination Unknown" by Missing Persons while a dozen gender illusionists and a dozen of their fans watched from tiny tables cluttered with cocktail glasses. Maxine sat at the lone unoccupied table while Rudy went over to the bar area (where a few garden-variety gayboys and two mannish lesbians ignored the proceedings) and ordered a pair of Lite beers. He returned as the song was ending and nodded toward the lip-syncher. "Diet time." Maxine smiled maliciously. Then the M.C., a highlighted, flight attendant type came out clapping and said, "Thank you Miss Minnie Sodapop from Minneapolis!"

"What an awful name," exclaimed Maxine. "So incredibly stupid."

"You're the one who wanted to come here," said Rudy. He didn't sound too put out, possibly because his eyes were busy undressing the next act, a skinny blond in hot pants and pasties.

Maxine sneered, "Who's that, Miss Ann O'Rexia?" Rudy said nothing.

Maxine took out her purse, removed her compact, and fixed her face. Then she surveyed the bar. The tragic blandness of the crowd irritated her. The contrast with the San Francisco watering holes of her youth, delightfully debauched neverlands full of self-invented weirdoes and one-of-a-kind dreamers, was painful to consider. The show ended after a few more forgettable numbers and the M.C. ordered everyone to clap for the best act. Rudy, predictably, went for Ann O'Rexia. Maxine threw her support for Minnie Sodapop. She had the best song and was the only performer who seemed to be having any fun. When Minnie came in third, she looked sincerely thrilled, squealing and covering her mouth with her hands like a game show contestant.

"Ready to go?" asked Rudy when the stage was finally dark.

"Let's have one more for the road," said Maxine. "And this time I'd actually prefer a Long Island Iced Tea."

Rudy swaggered up to the bar to order while Maxine went to the ladies room, a small over-bright space permeated with the smell of Juicy Fruit gum-scented disinfectant. As Maxine primped in the mirror, Minnie emerged from a toilet stall with a naughty look on her face.

"Loved your song," said Maxine. "It was nice to hear something with pep."

"Thanks," said Minnie, "love your dress. Would you like a little . . ." her eyes darted left then right ". . . pick me up?"

"Don't mind if I do!" Maxine followed Minnie into the stall and watched hungrily as Minnie removed a tiny baggie of white powder, a credit card, and a tiny mirror from her purse. Using the credit card, she chopped the powder into two little lines then pulled out a segment of plastic straw. After some rather unladylike snorting, the pair were high as kites. Exiting the stall, they began applying make-up in the mirror over the sinks with an unusual enthusiasm. Maxine invited Minnie to her gig at Big Louie's ("You're on the guest list!") and Minnie sobbed out her life story: she'd moved to California from Minneapolis with a rich cyber-savvy boyfriend. Moments after their plane landed, he'd left her for a gold-digging pretty boy who, she averred, was "thin as a swizzle stick."

Maxine felt a sisterly compassion. "Minnie, forget boys for a moment. We have to talk about that show out there. You were fine, but the rest of it was . . . not very good." If Maxine's verbal faculties hadn't been impaired by drugs, she'd have been able to articulate more fully her opinion that *the show was dull because all the queens were mimicking celebrities instead of creating new personas out of their dreams, desires, and the rich history of theater, art, and mythos bequeathed us by Western Civilization.* "You should move to San Francisco. There's more for a gal like you in the city."

"Like your boyfriend?" said Minnie. "Ha cha ha!" She fanned her face with her hand, as if cooling herself down from all the hotness.

"Actually, he's from here. What I mean is that queens in the city are—how to put this?—a little more *with it.*

Sharper, I guess you'd say. It's more stimulating. And as it happens, I have a room in my apartment opening up on the first. I'm right downtown, near everything really, and the rent is only five hundred a month. You could move in and we'd have a ball. I'm sure of it!"

"It sounds absolutely wonderful," said Minnie, whose addled brain was sparkling to such a degree that virtually any idea (possibly up to and including self-immolation) would have sounded absolutely wonderful. "You know, I work at Blondie's Pizza on Powell, so living in the city would save me a commute."

"Perfect!" squealed Maxine.

"But I guess you should know . . . I may be a total girlena, if you catch my drift, but I do mostly live as a boy. That isn't a problem, is it?"

Maxine manufactured a soothing chuckle. "Don't be *silly*. We sophisticated urban queens don't care what your *gender* is. So long as you look *fabulous!*"

Minnie smiled with relief. "Good. I'll give you my number and we can talk more tomorrow."

As Minnie rummaged around in her purse looking for pen and paper, Maxine's mind made a chemically abetted jump. "But you know, Minnie, you really should think about changing your name. Don't take this the wrong way, but Minnie Sodapop is too joke-y, even for drag."

Minnie pondered for second before agreeing. "I guess it made more sense back in Minnesota." She scribbled her number on the back of a receipt from Walgreens and handed it to Maxine.

"I'll help you think of a new one," said Maxine as she, lacking pockets, dropped the receipt into the bosom of her dress. "But I think maybe we'd better do another little line first . . . if that's okay."

"Sure," said Minnie. "I normally never do this stuff, but Bettina, the one who did Cher? She gave me some to get rid of it 'cause she's trying to give it up."

"Good for her," Maxine said. "Nasty, filthy habit." They re-entered the stall and did their business.

"Okay, what do I call myself," asked Minnie, sitting on the toilet seat and gazing reverentially at her new friend.

"Let's try the old standby, the name of your first pet and the street you lived on as a kid."

Minnie frowned. "That would make me Jingles Parkhurst."

Maxine clapped her hands in delight. "Perfect! It makes you sound like a madcap heiress."

"But I don't like it," pouted Minnie.

"What do you love more than anything in the world?"

"Let's see, Cheese Danishes . . . Barbie dolls . . . Justin Timberlake . . . noodles . . ."

Maxine rolled her eyes. "Girl, do another bump." Minnie didn't even bother with lines this time, just dug a little out of the tiny baggie with her pinkie nail and snorted, then let Maxine do the same. As they emerged from the stall once more, each stared at her own reflection in the mirror as they spoke.

"Okay," said Minnie, revving herself up. "Movies . . . cats . . . scented candles . . ."

"Not *like*," said Maxine, "Love! What do you *love?*"

Minnie shook with excitement. "Money . . . babies . . . men with bushy eyebrows . . . Moon Pies . . . That's it! I want to be called Moon Pie!"

Stupid, thought Maxine, *but better than Minnie Sodapop.* Anyway, she was feeling too good to care. "Very well, get down on your knees." Moon Pie wore a questioning look but obeyed. Maxine, using the liquid soap-dispenser from next to the sink, solemnly touched her new friend's right and left shoulders. "I hereby dub thee, Lady Miss Moon Pie. You may rise."

Lady Miss Moon Pie stood up and giggled. "How about another line to celebrate?" Maxine agreed that would be a good idea. They returned to the stall and finished off the baggie. "Oh Maxine, you're so much fun!" said Moon Pie. Suddenly Maxine remembered her date.

"Hey, I'd better get back to Rudy. We've been in here forever." She exited the stall.

"Bye honey!" said Moon Pie. "Call me tomorrow!"

"Absolutely," said Maxine. "And don't forget my show at Big Louie's!"

"Took you long enough," said Rudy as Maxine reseated herself at the table.

"I think I might change my name to Jingles Parkhurst," said Maxine.

Rudy's face fell. "Nah, that's . . ." He lacked the words for his objection, but Maxine knew that straight-identified guys into trans women generally preferred passing real-ness without any side helping of camp, thank you very much. Rudy leaned across the table and stared at Maxine's eyes. "Jeez, look at those pupils. You're coked to the gills!"

"What does that mean," asked Maxine, panicked. "To the gills. It makes me sound like a fish. Is it a fish reference?"

Rudy stood and glowered down at her. "If you think I'm taking you back to my place for seconds you're very much mistaken. What an asshole you are. Not only for what you're doing to your body, but legally endangering yourself, the bar, me . . ." A couple of passing gayboys stared wide-eyed at Rudy's outfit, then burst out laughing. He stopped speaking and looked confused.

Maxine had to repress a smile. "I'm sorry Rudy. Really sorry . . ." Before she could finish, Rudy stalked out of the club.

"Wait," Maxine called out, racing after him. "I'm sorry! How will I get home?"

"Not my problem, babe," said Rudy opening the door to his SUV.

"Be a gentleman," pleaded Maxine. "At least take me to the nearest BART stop."

Rudy sighed. "All right. Get in."

Maxine climbed in and endured a ride to the BART station in frosty silence.

CHAPTER 12

AFTER PARTY

Harris loved after parties and eagerly joined the small gaggle following Sasa up the street. He fondly recalled one from a dozen years ago during which he and his pals—still in their twenties and limber—had played several exceedingly sexy rounds of strip Twister. They'd run out of liquor by five and had to count the seconds until six when the corner store opened, at which point Harris had taken a pith helmet and butterfly net off the wall (whimsical decorations) and gone on a "wild booze safari." He returned with two bottles of "breakfast vodka" and became hero of the day. (Harris forgot to remember the end of the party when the overtired host had a melt-down and cried because nobody loved him, and everybody went home feeling weird and decadent.)

Harris was especially keen on Sasa's after party as, through the fuzzy din of inebriation, his brain was insisting quite loudly that Herb was utterly delectable. Perhaps he was a bit taller than absolutely necessary, but his youthful visage was classically handsome and his modest demeanor pleasing in the extreme. Harris surveyed the other partygoers to assess his competition.

Sasa: no problem there. Herb had cringed at his touch.

Vivian: biological female, no threat.

Lance: Though he would undoubtedly make a clumsy pass at Herb, perhaps several, Lance was out of shape and even older than Harris.

Roland: a hefty bar-fixture of indeterminate age wearing, of all the crazy get ups, a corduroy suit jacket. Herb would only go for him if he were into Daddies.

Curtis: a quietly gorgeous preppie type with (if the rumors were true) a sizable trust fund. Drat! There was no way Harris could compete. Perhaps, though, Curtis had a boyfriend somewhere. His sort often did.

Harris was deciding that, overall, his chances were fairly good when Lance ambled up. "Dibs on the F.M.," he whispered, pointing at Herb. F.M. stood for Fresh Meat.

"Dibs are fibs, one, two, three, no backtalk," said Harris, recalling the childhood formula for disallowing dibs.

"Okay everyone, make a left here!" bellowed Sasa. Moments later he was unlocking the door to his loft. "Make yourselves at home on my extremely chic Eames chairs for which I paid practically nothing while I see to the libations." He pressed a button on his CD player flooding the space with ambient chill-out music and went into his kitchenette.

"Oh my God, this place is so huge," said Harris, standing stock-still and staring wide-eyed about the room. "I've never *seen* so much space."

"It's a loft," said Lance. "Surely you've seen lofts before."

"It's like I'm seeing snow for the first time," said Harris, voice full of wonder. He then caught sight of the desk on which sat Sasa's computer. His voice turned acid. "And I see you've jumped on the computer bandwagon."

"It's hardly a bandwagon," objected Sasa as he stirred an elegantly shaped glass pitcher of martinis with a long swizzle stick.

Harris turned away from the offending machine. "I suppose you do the whole *e-mail* thing and visit *chat* rooms and *download* and all that." Harris sat down. "Pretty soon all socializing will be on-line and nobody will ever leave their home. I *loathe* computers and everything they stand for."

"Oh, I don't think people will ever stop going out," said Vivian. "At least not until they figure a way for computers to release pheromones."

Curtis peered at her through his wire-rimmed spectacles. "I certainly see you out a lot. Do you think this city is different from other cities that way? Are people friendlier?" He nervously brushed an imaginary crumb off his tan slacks.

"Hell yeah," said Vivian. "Compared to the rest of America, San Francisco is paradise. Where I grew up there were just all these *regular* people. Here I have my indie rock friends, my activist friends, my Burning Man friends, my queerboy friends . . ." As she spoke, she lifted her camera and focused on Curtis's face. "Now don't move. I'll immortalize you."

Curtis covered his face with his hands. "God, I must look awful right now!"

"No!" insisted Vivian, lowering her camera slightly. "You're really, really handsome. You have great cheekbones. If I was a gay man, you'd be just the type I'd go for."

"Hear that, Harris?" whispered Lance, poking Harris in the ribs. "*Curtis* is worried how he looks." Harris pretended not to hear.

"C'mon," implored Vivian. Curtis shook his head. "I could put your picture in my next gallery show so everyone could see how cute you are."

Curtis shook his head again. "Gay men are so wrapped up in their looks. I don't want to fall into that trap."

"Leave Miss Garbo alone," ordered Lance, preening campily. "Take my picture."

"Okay," said Vivian, adjusting her lens. "You've got a great face too. You've aged well."

Harris was unable to resist. "Yes, Lance. *You've aged well.*"

Vivian scowled. "If you ask me, gay men would be a lot happier if they learned to accept the aging process and embrace maturity. I was reading . . ."

"Wait!" interrupted Lance. "Get a picture of me with Herb on my lap. Come over here Herb." Herb shyly complied, awkwardly perching on Lance's knee. The camera clicked and the boy bounced back to his chair.

Sasa, tray in hand, began distributing drinks as Vivian turned to survey her potential models. "Now I want to take your picture . . . Roland is it?"

"Yes," replied Roland crisply. "But I do not care to be shot in this ghastly lighting. Sasa, you have a reasonably well-appointed home here. Are not your lights on a dimmer?"

Sasa sat down and frowned in consternation. "They really should be, huh?"

"That is not for me to say," said Roland.

"Now I know what to get you for your birthday," said Herb winningly.

"Heeeeeerb," mooned Sasa. "Isn't he thoughtful?"

"A treasure," agreed Vivian.

Herb pretended not to be paying attention but looked uncomfortable.

"Here we are, Boys in the Bland," said Lance. "In the good old days, we'd have shredded each other six ways from Wednesday by now."

"Those days don't sound so good," said Vivian.

"Amen to that," said Curtis.

"Nobody has yet addressed the lighting situation," said Roland.

Sasa bolted up from his chair and scampered into a closet.

"Let's all go back into the closet," suggested Harris. Nobody laughed.

Sasa returned carrying a candelabrum holding half dozen thin, white, candles, which he began lighting. "Herb, Sweetie, will you hit the lights?" Herb rose and complied. The transition to candlelight instantly relaxed the vibe.

As Herb retook his seat Curtis turned his way. "So what do you do, Herb?"

Herb again looked uncomfortable. "I'm getting an MFA in poetry at State."

"That's wonderful," said Vivian. "I went to a few slams and open mics last year. I admire their energy, but I'm not sure I like all that competition. Who're your favorite local poets? Do you know Michelle Tea? Bucky Sinister? Horehound Stillpoint?"

Herb all but whispered. "I don't know them, but I've heard them read."

Vivian continued. "What genre do you like? Who are your all-time faves?"

"New York School. Frank O'Hara," mumbled Herb.

"Why don't you read us one of your poems?" asked Vivian.

"Noooo," said Herb, reddening slightly.

"Such modesty," observed Lance with a smile. He tried to sound casual as he asked, "How old are you?"

Harris hunched over, gnarled his fingers, and put on a faux elderly voice, "Hooow oold are you, chiiillld?"

"Twenty-four," said Herb.

"Now don't be shy," commanded Sasa. "Read us a poem." He turned from Herb and addressed everyone. "He's very talented."

Herb blushed.

"It's so cute when he blushes," said Lance.

"Oh, I bet you could blush too under the right circumstances Lance, even if you are an old whore!" said Harris.

"I can't help it," said Lance, "My high school guidance counselor gave me a test and it turns out the only career I'm suited for is Old Whore."

"Please? Just a little poem," begged Vivian. "Even a haiku."

"I'd be interested," said Lance.

Harris felt a strong urge to inform Herb that Lance had no interest in poetry and had never voluntarily read a poem in his life, but suppressed it, not wanting to look bitchy.

"Have you read in public before?" asked Curtis.

"Er . . . I . . . no . . ." Herb seemed to have forgotten how to speak. There was a long moment of silence.

"Since nobody here has much to say it might be best if you did read something," urged Roland.

"Well, okay," said Herb. He trudged reluctantly toward the curtained off section of the warehouse that contained his loft bed and desk. "Just a short one."

"The length of a poem has nothing whatsoever to do with its quality," declared Roland.

"It seems like it might be harder to write a short poem than a long one," observed Curtis, who'd attended a small, private liberal arts college.

"Of course, how hard it is to write a poem has nothing whatsoever to do with its quality," Roland declared.

While Herb rooted through his desk, Lance picked up an old porn magazine from the coffee table and began leafing through it. "From these shag hairdos I'd say this is . . . '74?" He held up a photo in which a full-figured hermaphrodite in lingerie, wig ever so slightly askew, sucked on a lollipop suggestively.

Harris squinted at the image. "That hair is a variation of the Farrah. I'll say '77."

"Is this a game?" asked Curtis.

"You are both incorrect, it's obviously '76," announced Roland, his eyes fixed on the ceiling, his legs and arms crossed, his whole body radiating impatience.

"Who cares what year it is, she looks fabulous," said Vivian.

Lance checked the copyright. "I'll be a monkey's uncle, it is '76."

Herb returned holding a sheet of paper densely covered in tiny black letters and sat down. "Okay, here it is. I wrote it on the bus from Four Corners. It's called, 'White Skin Privilege on a Dark Night of the Soul.'"

"I'm leaving," announced Roland. He rose to his feet and marched out the door. The abrupt departure resulted in another long moment of silence.

"What was that all about?" asked Curtis.

"What a rudeness he is," declared Vivian.

Sasa rolled his eyes. "White people are so weird."

Vivian turned to the now ashen-faced Herb. "But *we* all still want to hear your poem."

"Yeah, go on," smiled Lance encouragingly.

"Yes, please," said Harris, who hated poetry every bit as much as Lance.

"I'd rather not," said Herb folding the paper into quarters and using it to fan his face.

Silence ensued.

"Any more boozerooni?" Harris asked.

"No," Sasa replied coldly.

"Here, have mine," offered Herb proffering his nearly full glass. "I'm not much of a drinker."

"No thanks," said Harris.

Vivian yawned. Then Herb yawned.

"Little Herb isn't used to keeping such late hours," said Sasa.

"I best be going," said Vivian, "Work tomorrow. Sweet dreams everyone!" She blew air kisses all around and swept out the door.

"She is soooo sweet," said Lance in a voice that made it abundantly clear he found such sweetness revolting.

Harris turned to Sasa. "I could really use another cocktail. Anything would be fine. Gasoline, rubbing alcohol. Maybe some old canned peaches in the back of your fridge have started fermenting. Go check, will you?"

"Give it up," said Sasa.

Harris put on a delighted face. "I know, what about your cooking sherry?"

"Don't have any," said Sasa.

"What!" Harris was indignant. "You gotta have some cooking sherry!" He wobbled into the kitchenette and began peering around. "Here you have this lovely loft, which you've done wonders with, and which is nicer than the places of oh . . . eighty or eighty-five percent of the places people we know live, maybe ninety, but you haven't gotten your kitchen together."

"Get me some ice water, will you?" asked Lance.

Sasa screamed, "Wait!"

Too late—Harris had opened the freezer. "Ah ha. Well, since you don't have any booze in the house, I can only assume this bottle with the Stoli label is actually mineral water. I think I'll have some *mineral water*, if you don't mind. I don't suppose you've also been hiding any vermouth?"

Sasa sighed. "In the cabinet over the sink. If you bring the voddy, vermouth, and ice in here, I'll mix up one more round of proper martinis." He put on a Mom-voice. "Then it's bedtime, and that's final!"

"Yes, Miss Lady Woman," said Harris, awkwardly (some would say insanely) attempting to transport the vermouth, vodka, ice bucket, and his glass all at once. "I know Miss Lancelotta over there wants more booze. And how about our lovely ingénues? Curtis? Herb?" As Harris stepped into the living room he tripped over a small throw rug, landing on top of Curtis, who made an ouch-y noise whilst ice cubes flew everywhere, and the two bottles hit the floor with a pair of thuds. Everybody squealed.

Harris got up shakily. "Oops."

Curtis held out his arm and whimpered, "The glass . . ." A small dollop of red was soaking through his white shirt where the stem of Harris's martini glass had broken and stabbed him.

"Poor baby!" said Sasa moving towards Curtis.

Before Sasa arrived, Herb leapt up, grabbed the injured boy's hand, and dragged him away. "We've got bandages and stuff in the bathroom," he said with calm efficiency.

"I guess," said Harris as he slipped into the kitchen to dispose of the vicious cocktail glass, "this would have to qualify as a freak accident."

"Freak's the word for it," said Lance.

Sasa surveyed the floor and squealed. "Ice cubes leave water marks on wood!" He dropped to his knees and began frantically collecting them.

From the bathroom came the sound of two boys splashing and giggling, followed by a silence that oozed romance.

Harris collapsed on a chair and smiled without mirth. "Oh, Lordy."

CHAPTER 13

NARRATOR'S MEA CULPA

IN OLDEN TIMES, AUTHORS COULD RELATE even the most sordid stories without fear of self-incrimination. Prevailing wisdom held that fiction was fiction and that was that. Alas, modern readers quit believing in impartial, omniscient narrators shortly after Santa Claus. Thus I suspect some of you are wondering why exactly I, your intrepid (if admittedly unreliable) narrator, am so very intimately acquainted with the affairs someone like Harris. Well, the shocking truth of the matter is that Harris and I not only moved in the same circles but were friends.

We met at the dawn of the 1980s when both of us were simultaneously hired at a small store in North Beach selling posters and postcards. During a lull on our first afternoon, we got to chatting and, somehow or other, started matching up Punk and New Wave singers with their archetypical equivalents from Old Hollywood: Siouxsie Sioux was an independent contrarian like Katherine Hepburn, Johnny Rotten a misunderstood moralist like John Garfield, Adam Ant a self-mocking dandy/sexpot like Errol Flynn. We got into an argument about Clare Grogan of Altered Images (was she Mia Farrow or Audrey Hepburn?) that lasted for two hours and really made the time fly. By the end of our first shift, we'd become pals.

Over the next few months, we took to going out on the town together, frequenting gay bars, repertory movie houses, punk clubs, arty cafes, and parties. Harris's social chatter was definitely above par, full of obscure cultural references and entertainingly bizarre factoids gleaned from his relentless perusal of hip magazines. I quickly discovered, though, that unlike most youngsters in pre-gentrified San Francisco, Harris would never invite you to his *thing*. He didn't play an instrument, paint, act, or write. What he did invite you to do was listen to his criticisms, which tended toward some combination of astoundingly harsh, somewhat astute, and entertainingly ridiculous.

This did not win Harris any popularity contests. At that time, San Franciscans strongly believed in being uncritically "supportive" of local culture. Why? Well, the city couldn't compete with New York when it came to media access. And nobody here earned big Hollywood bucks the way they could in Los Angeles. New Orleans would always outdo us in easy decadence, Boston in erudite intellectualism, and Chicago in broad shouldered populism. All that was left for San Francisco was to become the capital of Love and sweet-tempered sympathy. Everyone pronounced everyone else fabulous or brilliant, a tactic that ensured nobody ever got offended and refused to attend anyone else's *thing*, nobody lacked encouragement, and nobody ever quite believed a compliment.

This tendency toward mutual validation flourished most intensely amongst the starry-eyed bohemians of the city's underground art scenes. They (we) saw criticism as an assault on the sacred ethos of unfettered self-expression, something that depleted authenticity and promoted conformity with prevailing aesthetic standards. Yuck! Like the "folk artists" one might find in some remote mountain or jungle village, people produced art simply to please themselves and their friends. The results tended to be clever, self-indulgent, original, crude, whimsical, sloppy, spontaneous, off-beat, fun, ephemeral, and of little or no interest to that great beast, The General Public. Those who lived through the era tend to remember it as being rather magical.

Harris, however, paid underground artists the compliment of assuming they wanted not merely to be appreciated by friends and neighbors, but *to matter* in the big world outside San Francisco, maybe even to history. He felt the lack of critical feedback allowed too many to slide into a sort of pretentious mediocrity. Leaving an art gallery or concert he'd invariably shake his head with disappointment and solemnly deliver his verdict with a single word: "Reprehensible." "Pedestrian." "Sophomoric." By opting out of the civic habit of mutual back scratching Harris gained a reputation for negativity and was thus only tolerated rather than welcomed by his peer group. I minded him less than most because I felt his judgments, while admittedly over-harsh, were more respectful than automatic supportiveness.

Sadly, over the years Harris's taste for critical blood grew to the point where even I found his scathing reviews difficult to stomach. One noticed a shark-like glint in his eye as he offered observations and comments that were less insightful than just plain spiteful. This tendency toward hypercriticism was largely responsible for his paralysis. Having enjoyed the savaging of everyone else's creative efforts he knew, if only subconsciously, he'd have to apply the same unforgiving analysis to his own—hence his immaculate inactivity. The fact that Harris suffered more than anyone else from his hyper-critical tendencies makes him a victim as well as a victimizer, putting him, like Wolf Man and Frankenstein, into the class of pitiable monsters. Poor Harris!

One always pays a price if one goes about cavorting with monsters, perhaps frayed nerves, perhaps social embarrassment, perhaps ninety-two dollars. That never dissuaded me from Harris because—another shocking truth!—I quite enjoyed his company. I find most people blandly amiable to the point of insipidity, if not idiocy. Yes, it was draining to be around someone who persistently sought out reasons to be fearful, bitter, and gloomy in order to feed off the resultant negative psychic energy. But his bouts of amusingly absurd petulance and wild paranoia could really liven up a dull afternoon. Debating with him riled me up and filled me with moxie, dispelling my innate lethargy and keeping my metabolism on an even keel. The honest truth is that I used him like a psych-med or even (may the gods forgive me!) like *a party drug*. Oh, the shame!

CHAPTER 14

SUNDAY MORNING

MAXINE WOKE AT NOON FEELING PARCHED and leaden. *Why?* An avalanche of memories fell on her mind. Rudy, booze, Moon Pie, cocaine, public transportation. Propelled by hunger and thirst, she staggered out of bed. The refrigerator was bare except for some old but deliciously greasy Chinese noodles, which she devoured along with a glass of tap water. As she dressed, Maxine could think of nothing but coffee and cigarettes, neither of which she had on supply in her apartment. A quick search through her purse disclosed the unwelcome (if unsurprising) fact that she was flat broke. Though her monthly stipend would arrive in a couple of days, and of course she'd be fabulously wealthy as soon as Moon Pie moved in, she needed money immediately. Ugh! She'd have to sell CDs again.

First, though, she had to settle matters with Moon Pie. Big money was at stake, so she wanted to sound extraprofessional. She sat as upright as she imagined a highly paid professional secretary would sit at her desk on the forty-first floor of some gleaming office skyscraper and dialed. Moon Pie, who answered the phone as Dan, sounded trepidatious, but was still interested. She wanted, not unreasonably, to see the place before committing. Maxine opened her door and peeked into the living room. Harris had gone out for whatever it was a little troll like Harris went out for and the coast was clear. It was agreed that Moon Pie would come right over, though since she was bussing from Oakland and needed to eat first, she couldn't make it before three.

That gave Maxine just enough time to zip up to Amoeba Records to sell CDs. *I'm certainly paying my dues,* she thought as she wearily trudged to the bus stop. *This'll make a great story about the trials and tribulations I experienced on the way to stardom—like Tony Curtis living on ketchup soup before he made it in pictures.* She stared indifferently out the window as the 7 bus slowly trundled up Haight Street. Then, near Laguna, she caught sight of a Victorian house that flooded her mind with memories. She'd spent much of the 1970s within its rotting walls, laughing her youth away with the Summer Campers. In those heady days, before the advent of Gay Respectability, the city was liberally sprinkled with theater troupes lewdly and savagely mocking Mainstream Heterosexual America. The Summer Campers were far from the first or the funniest, but they weren't terrible, and Maxine immensely enjoyed performing their kooky comedy skits at parties and clubs. There'd never been any money to speak of and even the notoriety was negligible, but the whole thing had been fun, fun, fun, and given Maxine's life a sense of purpose and direction. She particularly grew to love the group's ringleader, Fanny Fishwife, whose gift for gossip, absurdly optimistic theatrical ambitions, and general exuberance never failed to lift her spirits.

And then . . . AIDS. Funeral after funeral devastated the group and its audience. Those who didn't succumb to the virus fled for the hills, hunkered down in their apartments, or traded entertainment for activism. The group didn't so much break-up as evaporate. After Fanny's death, Maxine stayed in her apartment for months, leaving only to buy red wine and snack chips from the corner store. She spent whole days in her bathrobe staring out the window at the unremarkable alley below. Occasionally she'd sing along with sad, old songs and look through the shoebox full of photographs and press clippings constituting the memorabilia of her showbiz career. Worried friends came by and asked if maybe she shouldn't try getting dressed, leaving the house, cutting back on the wine, or at least listening to cheerier music. *Something.*

Maxine patiently explained that she was comfortable in her robe and the outside world held no interest. Furthermore, cheery music depressed her while depressing music cheered her up. The knowledge that someone else was miserable made her feel less alone. Fanny would have understood instantly. And hadn't they heard? It'd been proved that red wine was good for your cholesterol. Ha ha! She didn't mention that her own brain was lecturing her nonstop: *The Summer Campers are over. Your career is over. You are not special. You are getting old. You are over.*

Relief and release from this tormented half-life came one night in a dream where Fanny was completely alive and spoke to her: *Look out your window. Does it all look gray and dull and depressing? Well, it is! But so what? The colorless killjoys don't own the universe! Why buckle under to the bores who won't accept you till you're dead and buried in some tedious job somewhere? Get outta bed and show some spirit! People need entertainment! Spread the gospel of good times! Go on stage! And no more drag circuit for you. You're a woman now. Go legit. Think Broadway! Think Vegas! Start now, while you're still young. Get out there and SING! You're going to be a STAR!* When Maxine woke, she knew her success had been ordained by fate. Better than fate: by Fanny!

And so, even at lowest ebb (and was anything lower than sitting on a smelly bus with a hangover on one's way to sell CDs for pin money?) Maxine felt an undercurrent of happy optimism. As she entered the record store she spied a magazine rack from which multiple models, pop singers, and movie stars stared out at her from the covers. It hurt her pride, just a little, that it was taking her so long to ascend from grubby reality to that glossy fantasyland. But oh, how she'd laugh when her time came and all the nobodies (like Harris!) got to see her looking flawless on the cover of some hip weekly under the headline, "Maxine Du Maurier's Rocky Road to Stardom."

With a few (measly) dollars in her pocket, Maxine returned to her apartment where she smoked and drank coffee until Moon Pie arrived. She was dressed androgynously in what could have been either a black casual men's suit or woman's pantsuit and shoes that looked like slippers. The pair air kissed like movie stars and Maxine gave the tour. "Here's my boudoir, here's the bathroom, here's the kitchenette, here's the living room where you'll sleep, and here's the hall closet which has a dresser in it that's *all yours!*"

"Apartments are so much smaller here than Minnesota," said Moon Pie wearing a trepidatious look on her face.

"And we're right near The Black Rose, where I met Rudy, the hunk you saw me with last night? We should go there for Brandy Alexanders to celebrate you moving in."

"It'd be nice to be able to walk to work," said Moon Pie, as though talking to herself. She opened and closed a drawer of the hall closet dresser in a businesslike fashion. "I can give you references from the last place I lived in Minneapolis, but not my place in Oakland. I'm there sort of informally and I'm kind of running out on my roomies. Ghastly people, if you want to know the truth." She turned and faced Maxine sternly. "And five hundred is no problem, I'm totally good for it, but I *can't* give you last month's rent *and* a security deposit. It'll have to be one or the other."

Maxine smiled. "That's fine, honey. No problem at all."

CHAPTER 15

HARRIS TAKES THE STAGE

PERHAPS I EXAGGERATED EARLIER IN SAYING Harris did nothing. Every so often he lip-synched at a weekly drag club. Subconsciously, Harris believed disguising himself as a woman precluded unflattering comparisons with masculine ideals against which he fell short. Also, he liked to pay homage to the designers of feminine fashion he worshiped. In no way, however, did he feel like a woman trapped in a man's body. As with many cerebral people, his psyche floated in a sea of words, taking little notice of the body to which it was attached. He never felt particularly gendered, except perhaps when drunk and wearing both high heels and something *really* slinky. Then, and only then, he noticed a certain swivel in his hips and a wiggle in his walk that felt unmistakably girlish. Let us now, through the magic of literature, view a randomly chosen and entirely typical night at the drag club for Harris:

Harris tottered into the club and headed for the bar, at which sat the hostess-M.C., Cupcake, dressed rather like somebody's Aunt Sophie all gussied up for a wedding reception.

"Praise the Lord, you're actually here on time!" said Cupcake.

Harris sputtered defensively. "I hope you don't think I'm *always* late. I admit I've been somewhat . . . tardy, shall we say, when performing here in the past, but not every time." He saw Cupcake's eyebrows arch with incredulity. "Or I may have been late every time I've performed *here*, but it's not my habit to be late for *everything* all the time . . ."

"Whatever, whatever, whatever," interrupted Cupcake with an elegantly dismissive wave of her elegantly manicured and be-ringed hand.

"Because I'd say I'm on time for at least ninety, or at least eighty-five percent, of all the appointments and commitments I have," continued Harris, "despite not having a car or a bicycle, though I did actually have a bike which was stolen, and having to take MUNI, which as you know is . . ."

"All right already!" barked Cupcake. "Thank you for your superhuman accomplishment of not being late. What song are you doing tonight?"

"'Is That All There Is.' Not the Peggy Lee version, but the New Wave cover by Cristina." He handed Cupcake his CD to pass along to the deejay.

Cupcake examined the jewel case and looked up with consternation. "Five minutes and forty-four seconds is kind of long. But, oh well, it is a good song. Let's see, there are ten performers tonight, I think I'll put you on second, okay?"

Harris nervously toyed with the long white feathered boa he'd worn to accentuate his white sleeveless A-line mini-dress and white vinyl go-go boots. "Well, as I'm sure you can guess, I'd prefer to go on later. Often people are still arriving when you go on second."

Cupcake's voice hardened with irritation. "How about third?"

"Well, it's not much better," sighed Harris. "But I guess I should consider it a privilege to warm up the audience for all the more accomplished and better loved acts that get to go on later."

"Great," said Cupcake. She whipped out her clipboard and wrote. "Act three, Miss B. Gotten."

Harris cleared his throat. "Also, I'm changing my name to Ann O'Mie."

Cupcake looked up from her board. "Huh?"

"Ann O'Mie . . . anomie. Get it?"

Cupcake's eyebrows arched. "Like . . . a sea anemone?"

"Anomie is a feeling of rootlessness, disconnection, alienation, or lack of purpose."

"Too obscure," said Cupcake with a quick shake of her head. "And kind of depressing."

"It's *my* drag name," said Harris defiantly. "And it goes with the feeling of the song."

Cupcake turned motherly. "Doll, this show business. You're entertaining people, not giving a vocabulary lesson. Rethink this."

"I considered Dee Moralized and Miss Ann Thrope, but I really think Ann O'Mie is best."

Cupcake scribbled the name on her clipboard. "Very well, but don't say I didn't warn you. That name is not a crowd pleaser." She handed Harris a pair of free drink tickets and stalked off. Alone at the bar, Harris surveyed the still thin crowd, the usual assortment of Good Time Charlies clutching extra-strong cocktails and chattering as loudly and meaninglessly as parrots. *None of these people would ever bother to perform, of course,* Harris thought. *But they'll probably brag to their friends at the office tomorrow that they went to a drag club like there's something hip and transgressive about just being in the audience.* Oh, how he detested them!

Harris then caught sight of the hunky shirtless bartender, Rex. *I suppose even a moment without having his brawny torso admired would be unendurable for him,* thought Harris. Then his disordered mind performed a little trick it had of thinking several thoughts simultaneously: *If I took my shirt off everyone would vomit/I hope Rex doesn't charge me full price for cocktails once I use up my drink tickets/I hope more people show up before I go on/I wonder what would it be like to* do it *with Rex?/Why does Cupcake hate me?* The conflicting noise from all these thoughts rendered them unintelligible, leaving him momentarily paralyzed. Then, as much out of bodily reflex as mental habit, he signaled for a drink.

Rex, recalling that Harris was stingy with tips, filled the drink orders of everyone he could before finally sauntering over and asking, "The usual?" Just as Harris nodded yes, a pair of adorably vivacious twinks scampered up to the bar.

"Oh, mister bartender, sir?" asked one, "A pair of extra-large Kamikazes, if you please." He and his friend giggled madly as if ordering drinks were the height of wit. Rex immediately filled their order, which he served with a flirtatious grin and a wink. Only when they had paid and left did he grudgingly concoct Harris's cocktail.

"Thanks," said Harris. As he slapped down his drink ticket, he decided not to tip. *He served those kids AFTER I'd placed my order, which is rude and unprofessional. And really, the only reason there are paying customers at the bar tonight is because of us performers. Rex should be tipping me.*

Drink finally in hand, Harris set off toward the tiny alcove, hidden behind a gold curtain and functioning as the backstage, but was intercepted by Vivian. "Miss B! That outfit is too, too fabulous. You look like a showgirl from some tacky exploitation movie starring Dean Martin circa 1966." She hugged him tightly. "Are you performing tonight?"

"Yes, although I was hoping to go on maybe next to last, or at least late in the show, I guess I'm going on third. Not to complain, but I've been doing shows here for years and I'm consistently put on first or second, third if I'm lucky, while some people, even for their first performance, get to go on next to last. I wouldn't ever even expect to get that slot because I know I'm not a 'crowd pleaser' as they say. I don't do the mindless, feel-good disco anthems people seem to want to hear. Still, I think that if I were ever allowed to—not even headline, I wouldn't even ask for that—but if I were allowed to go on later in the show, I might go over better because the people my act appeals to are, let's face it, the sort who arrive fashionably late . . ." He paused for a sip of his drink.

"Okay, Sugar," said Vivian, whose attention had clearly wandered "I'll try to catch your number. Break a leg!" She kissed Harris's cheek and scampered off.

Harris went backstage and stood nervously sipping his cocktail while running the lyrics to his number over in his mind. Meanwhile other performers wandered in, air kissed whomever, straightened their stockings, and fixed their faces in the flatteringly dim mirror. Finally, the spotlight came on, the music stopped, and Cupcake took the stage.

"Greetings labias and germs, I'm your hostess tonight, Cupcake. Yes, Hostess Cupcake." She rolled her eyes heavenward. "It seemed funny at the time. Anyway, we've got a bedazzling night of pure entertainment for you, so let's bring out our first performer of the night. . . Rhondamatic!"

"She's in the head," called out the deejay.

Cupcake put on a big, puzzled look? "She's giving head? To who?"

"The bathroom!" said the deejay.

Cupcake scowled. "How can you give head to a bathroom? Make sense, girl! Okay, whatever, whatever. We'll move on to our second performer, Annie O'Mie." Pause. "Don't ask me, I don't get it either."

Harris began loudly protesting that he was supposed to go on third, but his music was starting and Cupcake had retreated to the deejay booth. There was nothing to do but go on. No sooner was he standing in front of the half empty room (never half full, not for Harris) than he realized he was still holding his drink. He quickly set it on the edge of the stage and stood up with big smile. After a second of staring ahead with a frozen smile and terrified eyes, he managed to get into his prepared routine and mouth the old standard's bitter, alcoholic words. When the refrain about breaking out the boooooze and having a ball came on, Harris, as he'd practiced at home, took a long sip from his drink and pulled out a white feathered "fantasy mask" attached to a stick and covered his face while spinning around as if being waltzed by a phantom partner. This was his act's big (and only) shtick, and it did require some dexterity, but did the audience appreciate it? Harris suspected not. He also suspected that Cupcake was correct about the song being too long. It seemed quite endless, actually, and when it did finally, mercifully end, the applause was decidedly tepid.

"See what I mean about our performers being oh, just *ever so* special!" said Cupcake as she retook the stage, her hands making polite little clapping motions that produced no sound whatsoever. "Our next performer is our very own psychedelic princess, Alice Dee!"

Harris would have liked to relax after his number and bask in any glory there was to bask in, but unfortunately his mind was doing its little trick: *A nice soothing cocktail is in order/I've failed again/These heels are killing me/Cupcake is one mean motherfucker/If only I weren't so short!*

At the bar he waved down Rex, who pretended not to see him. Settling in for a long wait, Harris turned to watch the stage. Alice Dee, working a Hindi/hillbilly look with a Dolly Parton wig, bindi, gauzy sari, black cowboy hat, cowboy boots, thick leather belt, and scimitar, came out and lip-synched to an obscure dance-trance number full of banjos and sitars. A minute into her act, two extra pairs of arms belonging to her pals Noodles and Contagia shot out from behind her and started doing the multi-armed Hindu god thing. The crowd went wild. *Nice shtick*, thought Harris, *though hardly original.*

Just then, Wally's roommate Casey approached Harris with a grin. "Hey Harris, fun song!"

"Yes, well, I was humiliatingly bad, but thanks for trying to make me feel better."

"No, you were good," said Casey. "And that mask was a hoot. I went to Venice last winter and they sell them there for carnival."

"Wow, Venice," said Harris. "I hope you came back with a lot of phone numbers."

"Phone numbers?"

"Surely you made friends with some Italians while you were there."

Casey's smile faded. "Thing is, honestly, I was only there for a week, and I was staying in a tourist hotel with my mom, and actually the whole city is pretty touristy, so I didn't really meet any Italians . . ."

"Wow, you really blew it," said Harris. "I mean, Italy is full of fabulous people, you've seen *La Dolce Vita*, right? Fashion designers, minor nobility, movie directors. You could have made some friends and then you'd have a free place to stay next time you went. I don't know what you were thinking."

"We were just seeing art and visiting museums and churches and stuff. Just walking around is incredible . . ."

"Correct me if I'm wrong," interrupted Harris, "But part of the reason one travels is to broaden one's horizons, meet new people . . ."

"But we had fun. And the food was incredible."

"Couldn't you have just turned to someone at a bar and started a conversation?"

"My mom's not really a bar person, so we didn't go to any. Besides, I don't speak Italian."

"Darling, that shouldn't have stopped you!" Harris said in a jovial tone. "The people of quality *all* speak English. It's really too bad you went all the way over there and didn't meet *one* person. You'll just have to go back again and do it up right."

"We only could afford it this time 'cause my mom won some money at bingo," Casey mumbled despondently. "She's on Social Security and I'm still at Starbucks."

"Well, I'm really sorry," said Harris. "Maybe . . . maybe she'll win *again* someday."

"Thanks," said Casey drifting into the crowd with a long face.

The youth of today, thought Harris sadly, *are egregiously lacking in savoir-faire.*

CHAPTER 16

MORE MEA CULPA

HARRIS AND I WORKED TOGETHER IN the poster and postcard shop for a couple of years before I quit to work as a barback and he, shortly thereafter, switched to tele-marketing. We never lost touch, though, because San Francisco's gay New Wave scene was not terribly large. We were always running into each other while searching for the same obscure import record albums or striking rari-fied poses at the same nightclubs. We seldom ventured out of our insular little social scene, but our company was not missed by the larger world. Anyone observing us (some-thing nobody ever did) would've said, "Two peas in a pod." Eventually, though, a definitive difference between our characters revealed itself.

Whilst combing a thrift store for vintage treasures, I came across a Bedazzler, a smallish contraption for affixing little metal studs or rhinestones to fabric. During my youth it was marketed via innumerable low-budget commercials on late-night TV, touted for its ability to glitz up ordinary clothing. It had a brief run of downscale

popularity amongst overly craftsy moms and deluded dis-
cophiles, but by the mid-1980s home-bedazzled clothing
was considered the epitome of bad taste by virtually
everyone. So naturally, I bought it and began bedazzling
up a storm.

I started by putting little metal studs along the seams
of an extremely faded and torn pair of blue jeans, which
I wore to the Stud paired with a Joy Division t-shirt.
Friends asked me where I'd gotten the pants and before
you know it, I had a small business selling bedazzled
items to friends. I once added an ironic rhinestone
anarchy sign to a friend's jacket, and did a few penta-
grams for Goths, but mostly I just added studs to denim
jeans, vests, and jackets.

Harris was appalled.

On seeing my creations he'd roll his eyes and snort,
"Are you *still* foisting those hideous bedazzled thingies on
the world? I don't know how you can live with yourself. If I
were you, I'd be so ashamed I'd probably jump into the
mouth of an active volcano." At the time, I attributed
Harris's disdain to the fact he was going through a New
Romantic phase and favored only fancy, femme outfits
(his signature ensemble that year was Chelsea boots, Capri
pants, and a bolero jacket with a little metallic starburst
brooch on the lapel).

My crafting career didn't last long. Within a year my
machine broke and I, having grown bored with bedazzling, didn't bother getting it fixed. Instead, I bought a
camera with which to photograph lost shoes on the street,

eventually mounting a small show of my works in a café not much larger than a parking space. Not one item sold, despite extremely reasonable prices, and I quickly lost interest in photography. Thereafter I attempted, but quickly quit, rock journalism. Next up came a romance with Fassbinder films, which in those days could only be seen at repertory movie houses and felt very special. Then I took tap dancing classes for several months, giving it up when it became clear that neither of my two left feet was going to right itself. French cooking came next, but my soufflés always fell. I even (may the gods forgive me!) dabbled in performance art.

There were more enthusiasms after that, but I won't bore you with a recitation. This book isn't about *me*. It's about Harris and the pertinent fact is simply that Harris met every one of my enthusiasms with disdain. Whether couched as light teasing, serious criticism, or helpful suggestions, his objections to my efforts were generally rather incisive. Why would anyone want or need to look at old shoes? Fassbinder was fine, terrific even, but the fact I hadn't seen the films of Visconti was scandalous. Tap dancing was totally pedestrian, why didn't I take up Flamenco? French cooking was for social climbing '60s housewives. On and on. Totally wet blanketsville. And yet, whenever I felt I'd had enough of his mordant criticisms and vowed never to speak to Harris again, he'd surprise me with a bit of praise that was all the more valuable for being so rare. To hear from his lips that my chocolate mousse tasted "scrumptious" felt wonderfully validating.

If Harris disdained each enthusiasm for a different reason, there was one reason (never voiced aloud, but easily inferred from a slight rolling of his eyes and pursing of his lips) which applied to all of them—namely that I was *trying too hard.* I lacked what the Italians would call *sprezzatura.* (It's hard-to-translate, but if you say the word out loud in an Italian accent you might just get the feeling of it. Most definitions describe it as an air of studied carelessness or aristocratic nonchalance.) Harris was too neurotic to manifest *sprezzatura* himself, but he venerated it as an integral aspect of *chic.* I'm pretty sure my ambition and busyness offended him because it betrayed a sweaty, pushy, and unpardonably vulgar desperation . . . the very opposite of *sprezzatura.*

CHAPTER 17

SUNDAY BEER BUST

DURING THE 1970S, THE EAGLE GLITTERED darkly as one of the more notorious gay leather bars in San Francisco's sleazy South of Market district. When public raunchiness went out of fashion during the AIDS crisis a lot of the bars closed, some went straight, and a few tried to maintain their leatheriness with kinky theme nights and dress codes, inadvertently acquiring the air of live-action historical exhibits, little Colonial Williamsburgs of S&M. The Eagle, on the other hand, adapted to the winds of change by booking deejays and rock bands, drawing in leather-clad musicians to join the dwindling clan of leather-clad fetishists, and inadvertently creating a scene so eclectic it could happen *only in San Francisco* . . . or maybe New York or L.A., and if the rumors be true, Seattle and Portland, but probably absolutely nowhere else. The bar's Sunday afternoon beer busts always attracted leather queens, uniform freaks, pervy bears and otters, kinky activists, queer hipsters, circuit boys winding down from weekend-long chemical jags, and—strangely enough—Harris.

Walking out of the bright afternoon fog-glare into the dim, cavernous interior, Harris found himself momentarily blinded. As his eyes adjusted to the interior gloom, he made his way to the bar and purchased a mug of beer that would be filled continually by roving bartenders with giant pitchers throughout the afternoon. Just as he positioned himself against the back wall and took a first gulp, Wally emerged from the bathrooms. "What are *you* doing here?" Harris asked in a censorious tone. "And *what* are you wearing . . . or rather not wearing? Don't you own a shirt?"

Wally, who—though shirtless—wore a faded denim vest to match his faded denim jeans, reddened with embarrassment. "I'm trying to be sexually palatable," he explained. "You'd be surprised how hard it is to get laid wearing campy 1970s polyester."

"But, I mean . . ." Harris paused for dramatic effect. "Was it absolutely necessary to leave the house looking like some redneck grease monkey?"

"Redneck grease monkey is a sexy, sexy look."

"If you're going to wear a hideous vest like that at least you should unbutton it," said Harris.

"No way!" shrieked Wally. "It's hiding my love handles."

"Look around," advised Harris. "Lots of guys here are pleasantly plump, and more than a few have full on beer bellies."

"But I like skinny guys!"

"You wouldn't sleep with yourself if you weren't you?" asked Harris.

"Not unless I was drunk," admitted Wally. "Anyway, why are you giving *me* advice on cruising? I may be hard up to the point of desperate, but *you* haven't had a date since . . . Harris, have you ever, you know, *been with a man?*"

"Ha, ha," said Harris. He glanced up at a video monitor suspended in over the pool table showing a gaggle of "soldiers" grunting and doing lewd things with each other. "And these horrible X-rated videos. Why don't they turn down the sound? I mean seriously, must they moan like women in childbirth? Is that supposed to be sexy? I can't believe they think this is what we want to listen to and look at while having a nice social cocktail."

Wally grew exasperated. "Nobody's drinking cocktails, this is a *beer* bust. And since you clearly *hate* this place and everyone in it, why are you even here?" Then, embarrassed by his censorious tone, he put on an ironically detached smile. "You're harshing my mellow."

"I can hardly be expected to stay home with madwoman Maxine, can I? I simply came out for a drink, and I'm forced to view heinous acts of filth and depravity."

Just then, a tall, ruggedly handsome fellow standing amidst of a gaggle of ostentatiously buffed guys waved at Wally from across the bar. "That's Conrad who used to work at Kinko's with me," stage whispered Wally. "He left to become a paralegal. I'd kill a kitten to get him in the sack."

Harris scowled. "I see. You like *conventionally* attractive people."

"It's not like you get to decide what turns you on," said Wally.

Conrad disengaged from his friends and started making his way through the crowd.

Wally squealed. "He's coming over!"

"God, the 1970s bathhouse disco music they play here is *so* tired," said Harris.

Conrad arrived and grasped Wally's hand for a manly shake. "Hey Buddy, what's happening? Haven't seen you in a while!" The hand that wasn't shaking Wally's hand found its way onto the small of Wally's back.

"Hi," said Wally in a small, shy voice.

"Hey," said Harris with a bright smile. "I'm Harris, a good friend and soon-to-be roommate of Wally here."

"Pleased to meet you," said Conrad, shaking Harris's hand. He turned back to Wally. "What've you been up to?"

"I'm doing a play . . ." began Wally.

Harris cut in with enthusiasm. "Miss Wally's the queen bee of her own theatre company! Right now, she's playing a runaway teenage girl. What's her name? Dawn?"

Wally glared daggers at Harris. "Yes, but . . ."

"Right, Dawn," said Harris flashing a crooked little smile at Wally. He turned to Conrad. "Anyway, Wally's quite the drag diva these days. And he's got a show later tonight, so don't you be dragging him off to any wild and kinky sex orgies."

Conrad looked alarmed.

"It's not for *hours*," interjected Wally. He shoved his beer mug toward Harris. "Since you're heading up to the bar, would you mind getting me a refill?"

"Should you be drinking?" asked Harris. "What kind of an example does it set for your cast and crew if you show up to *your own* play drunk?"

"I'm not going to show up *drunk*," snapped Wally.

"I admit," said Harris, "That you usually hold your liquor pretty well, but not *always*."

"Harris . . ." Wally waved the mug in his friend's face.

"Aah," said Harris. "I get it. This is this a signal that I'm supposed to leave you two alone. Y'all are about to *hook up*. That's cool. You boys just be sure and play safe. There's a lot of cooties going around." He wriggled his way off into the crowd.

Conrad, his face a mask of dismay, looked to Wally. "Well, nice seeing you. I just wanted to come over and say *hi*."

"I *know*," said Wally. "Harris was just confused or something."

"Right," said Conrad with a decisive nod. "Hey, I should get back to my pals, see you 'round!" He vanished.

Wally worked his way through the crowd looking for Harris, hoping to inflict some variety of revenge. Alas, his quarry was not to be found. Though he'd been planning to stick around for at least an hour, he left for the theater early feeling vexed, dispirited, and furious.

CHAPTER 18

A FORAY INTO THE ART WORLD

AFTER MOON PIE LEFT, MAXINE WENT to a small, dingy corner market for some celebratory treats. While standing in the checkout line she heard a familiar voice. "Vienna sausages and Wolfschmidt vodka! Maxi you haven't changed a bit."

Maxine looked up from the magazine she'd been reading to kill time and gasped. "Gil? My God, it's been centuries. You look so different," The transformation from undernourished glitter hippie to someone healthy and well-groomed enough to sell real estate was rather startling. "But in a good way. Where've you been?"

"Guerneville. Remember Vincent? We got hitched. Happily ever after and all that. Gosh, Maxi. I don't think I've seen you since the Oak Street parties. Would that have been late seventies or early eighties?"

"Did Vincent ever get that inheritance?"

Gil laughed. "Maxi, you have a memory like a steel trap! Well, yes. Dear boy is fixed for life. We have this cute house on the river, our little love shack." Gil hoisted a dozen bottles of expensive champagne onto the conveyor belt as an indifferent store clerk rang up Maxine's purchases.

Maxine fingered the black silk of Gil's shirt. "Nice."

"Thanks," said Gil, taking in Maxine's vivid red wig, dark sunglasses, and kicky blue frock. "But I feel dull next to you. You've still got *sparkle*."

"Thanks," chirped Maxine. "Somebody has to. So what brings you to town? And what's with the champers?"

"Vinnie's having a show." He gestured at the bottles. "This is for the opening. The gallery was serving rosé, if you can believe such a tacky thing in this day and age."

"What's Vinnie's stuff like?" asked Maxine.

Gil whipped out a postcard invitation to the show and handed it to Maxine. "Very high of tech and brow. Come see, it's just around the corner."

"I'll try," said Maxine as she handed the cashier her money. Then, eying the champagne, "Oh, of course I'll go. I'd love to see Vinnie again."

As they walked to the gallery, it occurred to Maxine she hadn't seen Gil or Vincent at any of the Summer Campers's funerals. Fanny Fishwife. Paulina Peckerwood. Rabbit 23. Surely they could have come down for at least one.

"Here we are," said Gil outside of a newfangled building composed of corrugated metal joined at odd angles. Maxine stared through the gallery's huge plate glass door at a small, brightly lit room filled with soignée art-lovers. "VCG. Stands for Very Contemporary Gallery," continued Gil. "They're quite reputable." He pushed through the door. "Listen, I gotta deliver this bubbly. Vinnie's around here somewhere. Don't leave without saying hi!" He disappeared, wriggling into the crowd.

Maxine made her way to a pedestal on which stood what was presumably the art: a soiled diaper embedded in Lucite on a round disc with colored lights around the edges. "What the . . ."

Overhearing her, an expensively dressed middle-aged matron who looked to have recently had a facelift leaned over and murmured, "Push it." She elegantly gestured toward a red button at the side of the pedestal. Maxine did and the diaper began rotating while a manically happy children's version of "The Star-Spangled Banner" played from a hidden speaker and the colored lights flashed. The matron gave a little laugh. "Droll, no?" She walked away.

"Mary Mother of God," said Maxine. "That's it. Western Civilization is over." She grabbed a glass of wine from a passing server and downed it in one gulp.

"There you are!" said a voice from behind her. "Gil told me he'd found you."

Maxine turned around and saw Vincent dressed in a charcoal gray suit. Like Gil, he'd filled out and spiffed up. Unlike Gil, though, his face displayed a severity that had most certainly not been there back in the day. "Vinnie, congratulations!"

"Thanks," said Vincent. His eyes roamed up and down her ensemble. "You haven't changed one iota."

"You have," said Maxine. "In a *good* way. Oh, but I miss the old days. It was another world, a dream world, magical . . ." She suddenly felt moody.

Vincent arched an eyebrow. "Fun perhaps, but insubstantial. So what do you think of the art?"

Maxine delivered her all-purpose art review. "Provocative."

"The idea is that society's concept of beauty is predicated on an arbitrarily defined *other*, such as soiled diapers, which is used to perpetuate our concept of normality which in turn greases the wheel of commerce and promotes conformity. The clean diaper is normal, so *literally billions* of women spend *literally billions* of dollars buying diapers and *literally billions* of hours changing diapers. We're locked into an endless cycle of product consumption because we're afraid of our feces, literally scared of our own shit. It boggles the mind."

"Changing diapers is not very glamorous," said Maxine.

"You're missing my point," said Vincent with a tight smile. "I'm not saying anything about glamour. Nor am I trying to shock people. I'm questioning our society's arbitrary—and, to my mind, sick—dichotomy between bourgeois decency and filth. This isn't about beauty or the lack thereof, nor am I trying to expand the boundaries of what's considered beautiful. I'm questioning the very *construction* of the category *beautiful*."

Maxine chortled. "Speaking of construction, remember how you used to dress up like a construction worker to go disco dancing? You even had a yellow hard hat!"

Vincent remained mirthless. "Playing dress up is fun for kids, but I think we've all grown up a little since then. I'm trying to produce Art that *means* something. Art with a serious social critique."

"What's this supposed to be critiquing again?" asked Maxine in all innocence.

Vincent tried, but failed, to keep exasperation out of his voice. "Never mind." He paused and stared at the ceiling thoughtfully. "You know, Maxine, this reception is actually intended for people who might respect and appreciate my art."

Maxine's voice grew icicles. "You mean for Nob Hill snobs who might *buy* it."

Vincent's eyes widened with incredulity. "Are you implying I produce my art as a . . . a . . . *commodity?*"

"It is for sale, isn't it?"

Vincent opened his mouth, but only hemming and hawing came out.

Maxine declared victory. "Nice seeing you Vinnie, but I really must dash. Keep up the shitty work." She bolted from the gallery without looking back.

CHAPTER 19

DAWN: PORTRAIT OF A TEENAGE RUNAWAY

Harris had planned to leave The Eagle after a couple of drinks and head off to work at McWhitty. Alas, he never wore a watch and didn't think to glance at a clock until it was already quarter past five. Rather than going through all the trouble of heading downtown just to arrive extremely late, he decided to skip work and see Wally's play. *Might as well make him happy since we're going to be roomies.* It meant waiting around the bar (which was quickly emptying out and no longer fun) for another ninety minutes, but he could always console himself with more booze.

At six forty-five, Harris set off for the theater, a tiny, converted warehouse six blocks from the bar, and arrived ten minutes after the seven o'clock show time. Why it took twenty-five minutes for Harris to traverse such a short distance is a mystery, but Harris routinely defies the laws of physics by taking longer to do anything than any normal understanding of space and time would allow. (My theory is that he exists within that elongated species of time most of us experience only when waiting in line at the post office.) Once at the box office, the ticket taker informed Harris all the comp seats had been sold at five-to-seven as per theater policy. Harris officiously informed the lad he was the director's roommate and was resentfully allowed to stand in back.

The play was every bit as bad as he'd feared. Based on a 1976 made-for-TV movie, the story follows Dawn (originally played by Eve Plumb, famous for playing Jan on *The Brady Bunch*) as she runs away to seedy, sex-soaked Hollywood. There, she meets and falls in love with another runaway, Alexander, who, despite being straight as an arrow, is working as a male hustler. Too young to get a job, Dawn soon turns to streetwalking herself and eventually must be rescued by Alexander and a concerned social worker. Wally's play mocked this heteronormative set-up by implying that Alexander is actually a flaming queer sex-addict and had him go through the play wearing little more than scandalously short cutoffs whilst groping and being groped by all the male characters. Dawn, meanwhile, was depicted as an endearingly clueless cow. She spent the play changing from one hilariously ugly polyester outfit to another and murdering the already hokey dialogue. ("I wish you were a radio so I could turn you off!") This goofiness was made even sillier by the inclusion of choreographed disco dance numbers and cameo appearances by period TV stars like *Wonder Woman*, the *Six Million Dollar Man*, and Rhoda Morgenstern from the *Mary Tyler Moore Show*.

By the time intermission rolled around, Harris needed a drink as badly as he ever had in his life. The ticket taker was now selling wine and beer from the box office, but Harris was craving hard liquor and decided to run out and find a corner store. Outside, a low hanging fog shrouded the streets, caressing the cheeks of pedestrians like the ghosts of departed lovers. Or rather it would have, had there been any pedestrians. Though San Francisco boasted 15,000 inhabitants per square-mile, much of it was often nearly deserted. There were no crowds spilling out onto the sidewalk from raucous taverns, no hookers leaning against lampposts flirting with gaggles of off-duty sailors, no handsome juvenile delinquents loitering on door stoops singing doo-wop, no hobos warming their hands around fires blazing in trashcans, no children playing hopscotch or jump rope on the sidewalk, and no society types laughing gaily as they traipsed their way to swank cabarets. On that night, as ever, the streets South of Market were spookily deserted except for the occasional whizzing SUV.

Harris had to walk several long, desolate blocks before discovering a corner store. Inside, he found himself mesmerized by the variety of liquors. Which of these old friends would be his companion for the night? Saucy, impudent Jack Daniels? Classy, brooding Bushmills? No, it would be frolicsome, fearless Stolichnaya. While making his purchase, a wee, fussy-looking man with a familiar face entered the store. Harris vaguely recalled attending an opening at the man's art studio where he'd enjoyed not so much the paintings, as being at an event where he felt it appropriate for Persons of Quality to congregate.

"*Hiiiii!*" said Harris, who couldn't recall the man's name. "How's every little thing with you? Any shows coming up?"

"Hi Harris. No, I've been busy with my mid-life crisis," said the man, his elfin face smiling to let Harris know this was a quip, not a cry for help. "I fell in love with this kid and he's driving me crazy."

"When you say kid . . ." Harris began.

"Freddie is twenty-five years of age, perfectly legal," said the man.

"Then hardly a kid," said Harris.

"But a *young* twenty-five," said the man. "It's party, party, party all the time and merrily we go to hell."

"He sounds insufferable," said Harris. "I'd dump him."

The man stage whispered. "That's him out there." He discreetly pointed toward the front door, outside of which a rather fey moppet in a black trench coat stood smoking what was more than likely a clove cigarette with all the showiness of a silent movie vamp.

"Nelly little thing," observed Harris.

"That's how I like 'em," said the man. "So I can be the big, butch one."

The man's even, good-humored tone betrayed not a shred of self-doubt, but Harris smelled insecurity the way a shark smells blood. On hearing his friend's jocular admission, his face reddened in a facsimile of sympathetic embarrassment. He hemmed, hawed, and stammered, "Wow . . . you're so honest to like . . . *admit* that."

The man's sociable smile tightened. "Admit what?"

Harris smiled reassuringly. "Oh, I shouldn't say. Nothing."

The man's brow wrinkled. "No. Seriously. What?"

Harris's memory whirred into action, suddenly recalling the man's name: Jeremy Rabinowitz. "Well, Jeremy, *I understand*. Me, I'm not judgmental. But other people might think . . ." His voice trailed off ominously.

Jeremy cleared his throat. "Think what? All I said was, I like to date skinny little femme boys so I can be the big butch one." On repeating himself, Jeremy's face flushed with embarrassment. Was that weird? Wrong? Pathetic? The look on Harris's face assured him it was all three.

"Well, I wish you the best of luck," said Harris in a tone most people reserve for medical emergencies. "With your, what did you call him . . . your nelly boy?"

"I don't think I called him that," said Jeremy. "Did I?"

Harris put his hand on Jeremy's shoulder. "Take care of yourself, okay?"

"Later," croaked Jeremy.

By the time Harris found his way back to the theater, the second act was already underway. He would have hurried inside, but absolutely needed a cigarette first. The smoke break would be ever so much more enjoyable once he'd downed a little vodka, so he ducked around the corner into a shadowy side street to avoid detection by the roving puritans of the SFPD. He hated that his voddy wasn't properly chilled but made up for it by swigging from the bottle in a manner that a dashing private eye might take a nip from a flask in an old movie. As he stood, feeding his dependencies, Harris relaxed. Seeing plays, like partying in art galleries, struck him as classy, the sort of cosmopolitan thing the teenage Harris had imagined himself doing as an adult in the big city. The booze, the cigarette, the romantic fog, they all added up to Fine Living. He felt an uncharacteristic twinge of contentment.

Then, missing his usual comforting cocoon of anxiety, self-pity, jealousy, and sublimated rage, his ever-resourceful unconscious quickly produced some reassuring lamentations: *If only Maxine weren't out to get me. If only I were rich / If only I were handsome / If only this were Paris / If only Wally's play weren't awful.* He felt better.

On finishing his cigarette and almost all the vodka, Harris stumbled back inside and, ignoring the glare of the ticket taker, resumed his spot standing behind the back row. As he watched the play it occurred to him that he would be expected to thank and congratulate Wally afterward. Yes, custom would demand that he go backstage to express gratitude for his free ticket and distribute compliments. Well, he simply couldn't do it! The show was an embarrassment, an abomination. Words of praise would just stick in his throat. There was no alternative but to stealthily creep out before the play ended.

As Harris edged toward the exit, his right foot caught the back leg of a chair. "*Aiii!*" he screamed as he fell onto

the floor, bending his left arm the wrong way in the process. "*Ow! Ow! Ow!*" Excruciating pain subsumed his entire consciousness. Someone knelt beside him and asked in a whisper if he needed a doctor. Harris's mind couldn't quite compose itself yet. "It hurts!" A few seconds later the initial shock wore off and Harris regained awareness of his surroundings. People were staring! Terror and humiliation coursed through his veins. He scrambled to his feet and charged through the exit doors, which closed behind him with a loud bang.

Harris sat on the curb and, to anesthetize his throbbing arm, drank the last of his vodka. It took a few minutes, but the pain subsided. He could move the arm around and everything. Even so, Harris knew he had the makings of a great lawsuit. People were getting tens of thousands of dollars from injuries sustained in spaces that violated the safety codes. Clearly the warehouse theater was responsible for his accident, what with the narrow aisles and the folding chairs and the darkness. The most prudent thing to do would be finding a doctor to look at his arm and verify that it was badly sprained. S.F. General, however, was out of the question. The hospital's none-too-clean waiting room was—especially at night—a veritable hell of over-bright fluorescent lights, over-loud TV, and diseased indigents, many of whom smelled terrible and/or exhibited criminal tendencies. No, seeing a doctor would have to wait till the next day. In the meantime, since he had no desire to be at Maxine's place, Harris decided to go out clubbing.

Readers may be wondering how in tarnation Harris could contemplate yet more nightlife despite injury, inebriation, humiliation, and impending middle age. Some explanation is in order. There are exactly three ways for Party People to grow old. The first is to freak-out (with or without drugs) and leave town. Most town-leavers return from whence they came and are seldom heard from again, though a few manage to send cheery postcards one hesitates to take at face value. Could things really be "fine" in Columbus, Ohio? Harris would quite literally rather die than accept such a defeat. A few lucky leavers do find their way to Manhattan, L.A., or the Great Capitals of Europe, where *chic* is in the very air one breathes. Harris would have gladly relocated to any of those glamorous locales, but alas, lacked a small fortune, a car, or any facility with foreign languages. No, Harris could not leave town.

The second method involves Getting a Life. One returns to school, starts a career, finds a lover, acquires real estate, pets, and children, or at least houseplants. One's wild nightclub years become a curious footnote in one's curriculum vitae. This never occurred to Harris.

The third and final option is to keep partying in total denial. Ignore your back pain as you lean over to snort cocaine off some girl's mirrored platform shoe for a lark. Ignore your fatigue as you pile into a car with soused strangers to desperately trawl around looking for some party to which you weren't even invited. Ignore your boredom as you listen to someone half your age evincing the same archly-jaded cynicism you cultivated before he was even born. This was Harris's option. Over the next few hours, he did all of the above, along with other hijinks too dull to mention. Not till just before dawn did Harris finally creep home through the damp fog to rest his injured body and weary spirit.

CHAPTER 20

LOVE AND MONEY

Readers may be surprised to learn that I, Your Humble Narrator, am a shameless romantic. I cry watching corny old rom-coms, smother my pet hamsters with kisses on a daily basis, and firmly believe that all brides are beautiful. I do respect (in theory) my unattached friends's choices to remain single, but secretly rejoice whenever they find a partner. I'm not a traditionalist; I'm fine with promiscuity, open relationships, and asexuality. I just believe that everybody needs somebody to love, and have been happily hitched for years.

Harris, by contrast, was mostly prone to having small, squalid affairs with unsuitable characters. Where he found these odd ducks and miscreants is anyone's guess. Given their proclivities towards crime, lunacy, and indolence one suspects he cruised psychiatrists' waiting rooms or trolled behind dumpsters. The boys were always good looking enough, but definitely not take-home-to-mother-material. During these flings anyone who knew Harris was likely to get a late-night phone call requesting advice: "Jared borrowed the expensive camera my mom gave me for Christmas to take pictures in Golden Gate Park and says he lost it. Should I dump him?" "Antonio said he only needed to stay with me for a few days and he's been here for three months. Should I tell him to scram?" "Petey gets stoned and listens to prog rock. That's a deal breaker, right?" I refused to give romantic advice, but hinted it might behoove him to keep looking around for a better catch.

Then Harris started dating Carl, who seemed relatively sane and normal. He worked in an office, doted on his cats, and could carry on conversation—provided the subject was either David Bowie or the malfeasance of America's corporate overlords. Instead of phoning late at night with some ludicrous boyfriend crisis, Harris would ring up friends with invitations to join him and Carl at the movies or museum shows. I accompanied them on a few occasions and felt delighted that Harris seemed considerably less neurotic than usual. Then, just before the couple's first anniversary, Harris phoned me with a problem: he very much wanted to take Carl out for an anniversary dinner, but the date fell two days before his payday. Might I be willing to extend him a small loan. I, too, was broke, but unlike Harris, I was in possession of a credit card. Swept away by my romantic sensibility, I lent it to him.

When Harris dropped by to return my card the next day, he looked not just down or glum, but utterly wretched. Apparently, he and Carl had quarreled and broken up. He wouldn't say over what. Though I badgered him unmercifully, I couldn't get the details out of him. As for the ninety-two dollars that appeared on my card statement a few weeks later, I was unable to get that out of him either. And believed me I tried! You will recall that I, like Harris, am a gentleman living in reduced circumstances, a paycheck-to-paycheck pauper for whom such a sum was not chickenfeed. After my fifth or maybe sixth attempt to wheedle Harris into paying me back he flew to New York for a vacation. This so enraged me I vowed never to speak to him again.

The vow lasted eighteen months. During that time, I truly missed Harris's slightly cruel sense of humor, his unfailingly whimsical aesthetics, and his willingness to argue about virtually anything and everything. Perhaps most of all, though, I missed the smug sense of superiority I felt when comparing my problems, opinions, and lifestyle choices to his. On reestablishing contact, I did try one last time to arrange repayment, but to no avail. With a heavy heart (for I am petty and a miser) I gave up hope of ever getting my money back, though I never actually forgave the loan in case Harris spontaneously developed a sense of remorse and/or responsibility and decided to repay me.

CHAPTER 21

MONDAY, MONDAY

THE AUGUST SKY IN SAN FRANCISCO seldom displays
the pleasingly honeyed amber tones normally associated
with summer sunshine. Rather, it tends toward a cadav-
erous milky whiteness that depresses the spirit and
stultifies the mind, especially if the mind in question is
hung over, as Harris's was when he woke on the afternoon
of August 30th. After his usual lamentations, he heaved
himself out of bed and saw that (miracle of miracles!)
Maxine's door was closed. He slipped past it into the bathroom and performed his usual toilette as quickly as he
could. After that he phoned Wally, anxious to settle the
details of his big move. No answer. There was nothing to
do but get underway with his day. Task number one would
be rehydration. He felt like a dried-out husk.

Harris couldn't abide most of the city's cafes as they'd
been taken over by vulgarian dot-com workers in sensible
clothing. Fortunately, there were still a few spots where the
city's bohemian spirit lived on, places full of people who
scraped by working part-time at menial jobs while waiting

to make it as musicians, artists, writers, or comedians. In such cafes, everyone lounged with infinite coolness even as their eyes gleamed with white-hot ambition. Few of these people's names would go up in lights or down in history, but they all wrapped themselves in auras of potential and wore their hope like halos. Harris scorned artistic striving, but found it infinitely preferable to the sober industriousness of the dot-com crowd.

Waiting at the counter of one such cafe, Harris's eyes were inexorably drawn to the young barista. Almost handsome enough for a modeling career, the lad underplayed his physical beauty with a droll, *geek-chic* outfit of brown high-water slacks, argyle sweater vest, and a short-sleeved yellow dress shirt, all thrown whimsically off kilter by the cutesy pink plastic girl's hair barrette that failed to prevent several locks of curly brown hair from falling over his eyes. *What tired hipster thing does he do in his spare time?* wondered Harris. *Play banjo or theremin with some up-and-coming musical combo? Spray paint stencil art on freeway overpasses?* His sour conjectures were interrupted by a piercing voice.

"Harrisina!"

"Lance, please, not so loud," said Harris. "I barely slept a wink because I was grievously injured last night while seeing that ghastly *Dawn: Portrait of a Teenage Runaway* . . . Not that I ever sleep that well what with the insomnia from my chronic depression and . . ."

"Order?" interrupted the dreamboat barista.

"Small orange juice," said Harris.

"For you?" the barista asked Lance.

"Chamomile tea," said Lance in a hard-boiled manner, "And make it a double."

The barista forced a polite smile at Lance's jest and set about preparing the beverages.

"Hey," said Harris, tilting his head towards the barista. "He's kind of your type isn't he? All young and trendy and cute and stuff."

Lance poked Harris in the ribs. "Lower your voice, sweetness."

"Why don't you chat him up?"

"I don't even know if he's gay and he's definitely half my age," said Lance.

"Maybe he's a geezer pleaser," said Harris. "You'll never know unless you ask. C'mon, you don't want to wind up a shriveled old maid like granny here." He pointed to himself. "A withered, sexless crone without even a cat to keep her company. A scary old hag . . ."

Lance interrupted, "The ratio of geezer pleasers to geezers is not what one might wish." This last remark was uttered just as the barista, lips curled in disdainful amusement, set the tea in front of him. Clearly, he'd overheard. Lance blushed with embarrassment, grabbed his drink, and fled to a table.

"Thanks for leaving me to pay," said Harris a few moments later as he gingerly sat himself across from Lance and set down his OJ.

"You may recall you've owed me twenty-seven dollars since last year."

"If you'd owed me money for a year," said Harris. "I'm sure I would have forgotten all about it." As a diversion he added, "You totally blew your chance with that boy. Didn't you see him smile at you?"

"That was a smirk," said Lance. "I was utterly humiliated."

Harris sipped his OJ. "Oh, get over it, Mildred. Date another geezer."

"Not interested."

"You've bought into our society's shallow obsession with youth," accused Harris.

"You make it sound deliberate. Why would I choose to be attracted only to people who aren't attracted to me?" His eyes turned longingly toward the barista. "Besides, even if I weren't a hideous troll, there's no way I'd ever be *cool* enough for a boy like that."

Harris rolled his eyes. "You know the rules. If you're old and you wanna date the youths, you gotta become a sugar daddy."

"I'm not a *chickenhawk*, I'm a *hipster* fetishist. I don't want to *use* some young person's body for my own sordid sexual gratification. I want to feel that I'm part of a wild, sexy, and carefree tribe devoted to creative chaos. For an old goat like me, the love of a young hipster is the only thing that can create the illusion of such belonging."

"There are oldsters devoted to creative chaos."

"But they're not wild, sexy, and carefree. They have to deal with financial reality and the fact that their bodies are decomposing."

"You haven't got one foot in the grave *quite* yet, maybe if you moisturized, took up exercise, got yourself a cute little outfit . . ."

"Dressing like a club-hopping hipster twink when you're over fifty just makes you look even older than you really are. Not to mention desperate."

Harris sipped his OJ and put on a bright smile. "Well, I guess you're just doomed."

"Some oldsters," continued Lance, "do have some success by continuing to wear the outfits popular in their youth. You've seen them. Forty-year-old punks. Fifty-year-old flower children. Sixty-year-old beatniks. When your era gets resurrected by novelty-hungry designers and musicians, and becomes hip again, you suddenly seem like an endearingly authentic survivor from a long vanished golden age. The rapid recycling of trends means that, just as stopped clocks are right twice a day, you become fashionable twice a decade. The downside is that the rest of the time you look like an embarrassing dinosaur clown."

Harris, ignoring the stricken look on Lance's face (his eyes had taken on the dull, pleading look of a confined animal) surveyed the cafe. "Compared to the way we dressed back in the '80s when we were young, these kids actually look pretty normal."

"It's the cost of living," said Lance. "Because of the high rents, kids can't afford to go too wild. They rein it in so they can work proper jobs."

Harris snorted. "Our *wild* generation was pretty tired when you think about it. People disemboweling stuffed animals on stage while whining about their childhoods and calling it performance art, bands substituting attitude for talent. We weren't so great."

Lance shook his head. "Sure, there was a lot of crap back then, but at least we weren't so tediously professional. Nowadays the underground is awash in grant proposals and mission statements. The lowliest garage bands are hyped to the hilt on the internet and every protest or billboard defacement is carefully documented for posterity. There's been a complete reversal from the '50s. Today it's the patricians and petit bourgeois who're having wild sex, doing drugs, and allowing their primal urges to override conventional civility, while the counterculture types go in for poetry, knitting, sobriety, and community volunteerism.

"And I can't listen to these kids talk about what fuck-ups and outcasts they are. America's real losers are out in the boondocks. Most of these kids, even if they're cash poor at the moment from working crummy jobs while trying to 'make it,' come from decent homes. If they don't achieve artistic success by thirty or thirty-five, they'll drift off to grad school or lodge themselves in the office of some non-profit. They won't face forty without proper dental coverage."

"Lance," said Harris with a facsimile of real concern. "When was the last time you went for a walk in the woods? Go pick some wildflowers or pet some chipmunks or something."

"Not necessary," said Lance. "I've grown accustomed to my lonely solitude." He turned confiding. "You know it's been four years since I've had sex."

"Please don't tell me about your sex life!" said Harris. "If I ever fall asleep again I'll have nightmares."

Lance slumped sourly in his chair. "It's not my fault I can't relate to today's youth. There's a gay generation gap. We came out back when being out meant spending life on society's margins. And people like you and me were even marginal on the gay margins because we preferred the Ramones and Joy Division to Bette Midler and Donna Summer. Young gays have no idea what it's like to be completely marginalized. Of course, they don't have it easy in other ways. I paid nothing for rent in my twenties and living was cheap. Nowadays kids have to give up their artistic dreams if they don't pay off or they could end up *literally* homeless."

"You're forgetting," said Harris, "that half these kids don't have economic pressures, they have trust funds."

Lance, who'd squandered a medium-sized inheritance, became defensive. "What's your point?"

"It's not good for the arts," said Harris. "Rich kids pretty much *run* the avant-garde and it's become immature and elitist. If I'd had a little money, I could have gone a lot farther in life. Instead of spending all my energy trying to survive I could have focused on my career as a fashion designer."

"Seems to me," said Lance, "that hipsters from the wrong side of the tracks usually do better than their upper-class friends. They're more motivated."

"My dad taught Spanish at a community college and my mom was a bank teller," said Harris, his eyes misting over at the tragic injustice of it all. "I had plenty of motivation. I didn't want to wind up like them, slaving away just to survive. I wanted to be a designer, but nobody ever offered to fly me to New York and pay my way to fashion school. Hey, didn't you get sent to the Art Institute?"

"I went to the Art Institute for a few semesters," said Lance.

"Your rich parents paid for you to go to the Art Institute," continued Harris. "But you dropped out, right?"

Lance sighed. "Your point?"

"You blew it," said Harris. "You could have done something with your life."

"I have done something, I'm a painter-slash-waiter."

"In other words," said Harris, with relish, "a bum."

Lance sighed. "Becoming a bum is the best thing a rich kid can do for the poor."

Harris scowled. "How so?"

Lance launched into a well-rehearsed monologue. "We all know rich kids have advantages: nepotism, trust funds, connections, educations. If Little Brendan Whatever the Third shows the slightest talent with his toy tuba he's whisked off to a prestigious music academy, while Joey Average, should he display aptitude with the annoying plastic trumpet Mama's boyfriend brought home from the sports arena, will simply be given a baloney sandwich and asked to play outside. But if little Brendan drops out of said music academy because he's busy experimenting with Eastern mysticism and psilocybin, it opens a slot for Joey. It's the same in business. Daddy's firm won't fold because

Brendan is too busy making underground movies or tribal trance music to take over as CEO, it will simply hire from within. Positions at elite universities and upper-class jobs will be filled one way or another, if not with rich kids, then with strivers from the lower orders. Downwardly mobile rich kids make upward mobility possible."

"Only you," sneered Harris, "would try to turn being a deadbeat into a noble cause. Anyway, even if you don't want to be professional you could at least try to be a success. It's like you seek out failure, exhibiting your paintings in coffee houses and hair salons. Where's that going to get you?"

Lance bridled. "It's not so easy to get gallery shows. Besides, everyone knows artists often aren't discovered in their own lifetime. See if my paintings aren't all the rage in a hundred years."

"If you compare yourself to Vincent Van Gogh, I will be forced to slaughter you with my bare hands," said Harris. "I have my limits."

"You should pity us poor, aging, failed artistes," said Lance (cleverly removing all the aforementioned epithets from Harris's arsenal of insult by using them himself). "Resigned from the rat race, we face maturity without fame, money, respect, or the mental discipline necessary to face working nine to five. We become a wraithlike fraternity of old ghosts haunting the playgrounds of youth as our faces and bodies sag under the unbearable weight of thwarted ambition, boredom, and disappointment."

"I hope you're not including me in this," said Harris.

"You have never failed," observed Lance, "Only because you have never tried."

Harris suddenly remembered his very engrossing personal drama. "So, as I mentioned, I was injured last night. I went to see Wally's tired play and, as I was leaving, one of their chairs tripped me and I sprained my arm."

"It doesn't look sprained," said Lance. "You're moving it around."

"I'm just about to go get it looked at now," said Harris. He glanced at the clock, which read 3:20. "Or, actually, I'll probably have to go tomorrow. I blew off work last night to see that dramatic travesty and forgot to call in, so I'd better not miss work again tonight. Of course, when I explain about my arm they'll probably be very sympathetic, though I suppose I should find a sling because I don't want to injure it any more than I already have . . ."

"Okay, okay, okay!" said Lance. "Go to work already!"

CHAPTER 22

BOILER ROOM

HARRIS PUSHED THROUGH THE GLASS DOORS of McWhitty Market Research with the stoic fatalism of an aristocrat marching to the guillotine. Stan, the thin, nervous, and abnormally desiccated man who managed the phone room, stood sentry at the front desk.

"Hi Harris. I hope everything's okay." He smiled wanly, as if embarrassed, while his left hand fluttered and weaved, as if unsure what to do with itself. "We missed you yesterday. You know you're supposed to call if you can't make it in." The hand finally settled on running itself through Stan's thin gray-blond hair.

"I was in an accident," explained Harris. "I sprained my arm." He held the arm up for Stan's inspection. "I was in excruciating pain and . . ."

"Oh, that's too bad," cut in Stan. "We're already half an hour into the shift so you should really get started."

Harris glanced at the clock, which read 5:55, and decided he wouldn't apologize for being a mere twenty-five minutes late, especially since he was injured. "Okey dokey!"

he said, unconsciously imitating one of Stan's favorite expressions. He would have liked a smoke break, but since he was only paid one dollar for every survey he conducted, on top of the paltry six-dollars-an-hour base pay, he decided he'd better start phoning. In the best of circumstances, it was hard to get more than three surveys done in an hour and he was already behind.

How did I wind up working with such losers? wondered Harris as he walked down the aisle of cubicles. There was Leena, an elderly New Yorker with a voice like a buzz-saw; Constance, the immaculately dressed African American woman forever rolling her eyes in outraged disbelief; Caroline, a dowdy woman prone to sneaking peeks at a tiny bible she kept in her purse; and a punky college kid named Paul or David (Harris could never remember) who was cute, but almost certainly straight. *I've lost life's lottery.*

Harris sat at his cubicle, lined with gray, sound-absorbent carpeting, and switched on the computer monitor. He typed in his password, donned his headset, and held his pencil poised over the first page of a blank, fourteen-page survey as he waited for the auto-dialer to connect him. The first respondent was, the data screen informed him, Grace Robertson of Stockton, a city Harris had never visited, but suspected to be a vulgarian hellscape full of rednecks on crystal meth and religious fundamentalists.

"Hello?" said a woman as a child screamed unmercifully close to the receiver. "To whom am I speaking?"

"My name is Harris and I'm calling from McWhitty Market Research on behalf of Lady L'amour cosmetics. Have I reached Grace Robertson?"

"You most certainly have!" cried Grace happily. When Harris began working the phones, nothing had surprised (and depressed) him more than the existence of people whose lives were so dull they welcomed his calls.

"This will only take a few brief moments of your time, and I'm not selling anything. We're conducting a survey to gauge customer satisfaction so we can better serve you with our products. This call may be monitored for quality control."

"I love Lady L'amour cosmetics! I buy them all the time, oh . . . that must be how you got my name, from the warranty on my Romantasy Red lipstick. My girlfriend Rhonda says it's silly to fill out a warranty on lipstick, but I say you never know."

In the background Harris heard a male voice. "Where's the Spaghetti-Os?" Harris shuddered, remembering their sweet, metallic taste from childhood.

Grace bellowed, "In the cabinet right in front of you!"

"Do you, or does anyone in your family, work for Lady L'amour or any market research firm?" asked Harris.

"Nope," said Grace as in the background her children sang a cloying commercial jingle: *Give us, give us, sumpin' ta eat/howzabout, a puddin' snack treat?*

"Great," intoned Harris, robotically. "Let's start. Would you agree or disagree that Lady L'amour is an up-to-the-minute brand for trendsetters?"

"Agree," said Grace. "And could you speak up, it's noisy in here."

"Okay!" said Harris. "Would you say you strongly agree, or only somewhat?"

"Strongly," said Grace. There was a small crash in the background.

"Now, thinking about Lady L'amour beauty products . . ."

"What?" Grace asked. "I still can't hear you."

"Thinking about Lady L'amour beauty products! Would you say! That Lady L'amour foundation! Is too creamy! Just right! Or not creamy enough?!"

"I don't know. I don't especially care how creamy it is. Can I say that?"

"If you had to chose one . . ."

"How long does this survey go on? My family is ready to eat."

"Just a few more questions," lied Harris, his profound boredom only mitigated by the terror he felt at living in a world where this abomination of a job could even be allowed to exist.

Grace sighed. "Okay. What was the question again?"

Eight terrible minutes later, Harris finished.

Stan walked up to his cubicle. "Good job Harris, I guess that woman was a little deaf."

"Yes," said Harris, too emotionally exhausted to explain about the noisy family.

Stan picked up the survey and began leafing through it. "Oh dear. You missed question 14 C, the one about lip-gloss. You're going to have to call her back."

Harris fabricated. "Oh, she said translucent. I'm sure she did. I just forgot to write it down."

"We have very explicit instructions from Lady L'amour about this. All answers have to be written down *while you're on the phone* or we can't use the survey."

Harris grabbed the survey without a word and hit the redial button on the computer keyboard. A male voice answered. "Who's this? We're having dinner."

"My name is Harris and I just spoke with . . ."

"You that survey guy? Don't call here ever, ever again!" The computer screen flashed the word DISCONNECT.

"Oh, too bad," smiled Stan consolingly, "we won't be able to use the survey." He picked up the survey from Harris's desk and threw it in the recycling bin on the way back to his office. Harris, while visualizing a fiery death for Stan, forced himself to resume calling.

Break time came at seven. After a quick smoke in front of the building, Harris slumped into the break room and began rummaging around the snack station, a cabinet full of saltine crackers, instant soup mix, and stale chocolates. Harris felt starved, but all the food looked repulsive. The chocolate Easter eggs were slightly tempting, but it struck him as somehow blasphemous to eat them in August.

Paul-or-David came in and grabbed a packet of chicken noodle soup mix. "I thought you were a vegetarian," said Caroline as he emptied a package into a mug.

"I am," said the boy as he added hot water, "But there's only like one millionth of a chicken in here. I bet Lipton hasn't had to kill a new chicken since 1982. I don't think it'll matter karmically."

"Karmically!" said Caroline with a manufactured chuckle. "You're a funny one."

The smell of the soup, not appetizing by any means but definitely that of an edible substance, overcame Harris's reluctance. He fixed himself a mug, blew on it and took a sip. The chemical flavor invaded his mouth like the Nazis entering the Sudetenland, welcomed but with a faint foreboding of terrible evil. He sipped again, then emptied the mug into the sink, realizing there was no way he could stomach such an inferior product.

Meanwhile Leena, sitting resignedly in front of a bowl containing a pale liquid, addressed the room. "My doctor says I should cut out all fat, so here I sit eating tasteless vegetable broth. No flavor. None. Zip. You think my doctor avoids fat? To look at him you'd think he lives on beef and bonbons. The man is enormous. All blubber."

Constance, daintily eating from a plastic box of salad, chimed in. "Ain't it the truth? The doctors, they look worse than anybody. Where do *they* get the nerve to tell *us* what to eat?"

Leena nodded in vigorous agreement. "And we pay them for it! Good money! I go in for my allergies, talk to the man for five minutes and the bill comes to half a week's salary! This country needs socialized medicine. You know how much the CEO of a typical insurance company makes?"

"More than I do, that's for sure!" laughed Constance. "And I work two jobs. It's killing me. I'll be in my grave before the year's done."

"That's capitalism for you," said Leena. She took a loud slurp of broth. "If we can't have a revolution, we at least need a union."

"They'd move operations to India so fast it'd make your head spin," said Paul-or-David with a sad shake of his head.

Constance nodded. "My cousin Lester's in a union. Y'know how much he makes an hour?"

Before anyone could venture a guess, Stan skulked into the room. "Hi everybody. First, I'd like to congratulate you all on what a great job you're doing tonight. We've got twenty-nine surveys done already, so it looks like we'll make quota. That's really excellent and you all deserve a pat on the back." He beamed a happy smile, paused, then put on a graver face. "Unfortunately, I've got some bad news. The company's looking for a place to make some cutbacks and I hate to say . . . they're considering the snack station. I know it'd be a real blow because we all like to come in here and have a little snack during our break, but it is a privilege, not a right. Of course, even if we lose the station, we'll still have the vending machines. And you can still keep your own food in the fridge."

Caroline, oozing obsequiousness, spoke first. "Thanks for telling us personally, Stan. I know the snack station was your baby and we all really appreciate it."

Leena, who'd never actually eaten anything from the

snack station, sat upright and peered incredulously at Stan. "Are you saying . . ." she began in long, measured tones, "that *our* snack station is to be no more? Poof, just like that, we're *losing* the snack station?"

Stan's hands began fluttering. "What I said was, they're considering . . ."

"I'm considering something too, an' that's walking right outta here," muttered Constance.

"Exactly how much would they save from canceling the snack station?" asked Leena. "And whose decision is this exactly?"

Stan leaned against the table in what he imagined was a casual manner. "I don't have actual figures in front of me, and anyway, nothing's been decided for sure. I'm just letting you know that it's under consideration. And I'm definitely going to go to bat for the station. You all work very hard and I think you deserve it."

Leena's eyes shone with fire. "Good, because if that's an example of the high regard in which the senior management holds us . . ." Her voice trailed off ominously.

"Don't worry too much Leena, I think they'll see reason when I explain to them how much it means to all of you." Though definitely not a team player, Leena routinely completed six or more surveys an hour. Without her, meeting the room's quota would be nearly impossible. A fact of which both she and Stan were well aware.

"When exactly will they be making the decision?" asked Leena, folding her arms over her chest in an unmistakable display of social dominance.

"I'll get back to you as soon as I know anything more," said Stan with a terrified smile as he fled the room. Leena and Constance resumed their grumbling with renewed fervor as Caroline smiled at Harris in commiseration. "I hope they keep the station. A little chicken soup is good for the soul."

Harris tried to speak, but everything he wanted to say would be too bitter and negative to utter in front of Caroline. (Must we count it in his favor that Harris took no pleasure in parading his sophisticated cynicism before simple folk? I think we must.) "Yeah, I guess they say that," were the words he finally forced through his mouth.

"You know what I always say?" Caroline's voice went sing-song, "When times are bad and getting worse, keep a cookie in your purse!" She dug a grotesquely fat, pale cookie covered in M&Ms out of her large purse and held it out to Harris. "I baked it myself."

"Thanks," said Harris, taking the cookie and wrapping it in a napkin. Caroline gave him a wink and preceded him through the door back into the phone room. Harris threw the cookie in the trash and walked back toward his cubicle. His feet, however, redirected him to Stan's desk.

"Hi Stan. I hate to say this, but I don't think I'm feeling quite up to par. My arm is starting to throb, and it's throwing off my concentration."

"Oh, that's too bad," said Stan. "I know it's hard to work when you're not feeling your best, when you can't give a hundred percent."

"I think I'm more like at forty or maybe even thirty-five percent," said Harris.

"If you leave it'll negatively impact our chances of reaching quota tonight."

"I'm really sorry. I'm sure I'll be back to normal by tomorrow."

"Very well," said Stan with an ominous glower, "I'll see you tomorrow."

CHAPTER 23

MAXINE SINGS

Maxine admired herself in the mirror. Her long, tight black dress had a white marabou collar and cuffs that made her look like a kept woman from the Edwardian era crossed with a Dr. Seuss animal. She stood up and swished this way and that. *Spectacular!* As she fiddled with her hair, Maxine reluctantly admitted to herself that she missed her lady-in-waiting. Longing for a word of encouragement, she dialed Andy All Star, but found his phone disconnected. This was no real cause for worry as he led a rock 'n' roll lifestyle and was prone to lapses of basic competency. It was annoying, though, as she'd hoped to get a ride to the gig in his van. The idea of taking the bus was too gruesome to contemplate, so she called a cab, wiping out the last of her funds.

Big Louie's sat on the border between the rundown but trans-friendly Tenderloin and fancy-shmancy Nob Hill. It had opened in the 1930s as an Art Deco masterpiece, but over the years indifferent owners had thoughtlessly remodeled, allowing it to sink into sports bar mediocrity. The regular clientele changed accordingly from dapper swells tippling pre-show hi-balls to lowlife alkies hunched over beers and rotgut well drinks. The latest proprietor, sick of cleaning up riff-raff's vomit in the bathroom, let Maxine convince him she could bring in a higher class of customers with monthly performances. There was no stage, but she could stand or sit on the bar. Monday nights were dead anyway.

Maxine swept into Big Louie's with a hollered "Hello!" that caused several of the sodden regulars to jump half out of their skins. Andy All Star, dressed à la Johnny Cash in countrified black, was already sitting at the bar. On seeing her he, immediately pointed to the bartender. "Tell him I get free drinks!"

Why must there always be this absurd haggling over something as common as alcohol? Maxine wondered. "Calm yourself down. I'll take care of it," she said. "And lose the hat."

"Covers my bald spot," whispered Andy.

"Baldness is a sign of virility," said Maxine. "And cowboy hats are simply not *credible* on mama's boys from Marin." Andy sighed and removed the hat. Maxine smiled and spoke with the bartender. Once she'd procured vodka tonics for herself and Andy, she sat down to await show time while Andy set up a mic stand and a small amp in the corner.

Years of performing around town had given Maxine a small but solid fan base of arty, intellectual gay guys. Embracing Maxine as one's favorite diva was a badge of good taste amongst this tiny tribe for the very good reason that she possessed, along with an interesting voice and zany fashion sense, a thrillingly erudite song repertoire. When a Republican was in the White House and talk was of insipient fascism, Maxine would trot out songs from *Cabaret* or Brecht and Weill, evoking Weimar Germany. When times were good, she'd switch to British Invasion, '60s bubblegum, or Broadway. Sultry summers found her leaning toward sexy Southern swamp rock, and lonely holiday seasons brought out plaintive rockabilly ballads or complexly miserable Scott Walker tunes. She'd even, with Andy, written some of her own songs, which were also greatly appreciated by the cognoscenti.

This particular evening, Maxine's audience contained an underground film director, two drag divas, a failed novelist, a club promoter, a journalist for one of the free weekly gay papers, a drug dealer, a pair of avant-garde jewelry designers, a half-dozen underemployed yet still somehow rather *chic* boozehounds, and your humble narrator. As the attendees traipsed in, each offered Maxine words of support, for these were pals as well as fans. Ralph and Jasper, unsurprisingly, failed to show up, but Moon Pie, dressed in her androgynous suit, did. After greeting each other with a quick hug, the pair made their deal official: Maxine handing over her spare set of keys and Moon Pie handing over a white envelope. Maxine had just enough time to open it up and marvel at the check inside. A thousand dollars! A couple of well-wishers came over to greet her as she did this, forcing her to quickly put the check away in her purse. Moon Pie retreated shyly to a corner to await the show.

When it came time to begin, Maxine took the mic out of the stand and hoisted herself up onto the bar, positioning herself under one of the track lights. Channeling Marlene Dietrich, she crossed her legs seductively and addressed the audience. Not having an M.C. to introduce her was embarrassing, so she struck a comically casual tone. "Okay, I'm starting now. You all have to shut up and listen!" The crowd quieted. "This is a little number I wrote myself called 'Trash Floats.'" She nodded to Andy, tucked away in his dark corner, and he started to play as she sang:

> The rulers of the world/Are stupid and mean
> I'm sure they all deserve/The guillotine
> The speeches they make/And the clothes that they wear
> And the horrible things/That they do to their hair
> Human nature/Fills me with gloom
> I'd like to complain/But I'm not sure to whom
> No second coming/No revolution
> Offers me/Much of any solution
> Yet in the rising tide/Of devastation we see
> All sinks, but trash/Which floats clear and free
> So friend, be like refuse/Be like trash and survive
> Lose your morals and hopes/Be like garbage and thrive!

The intimacy of the space, lack of stage, and relentless Bohemianism of the audience combined to create an informal cabaret vibe, so after Maxine's first number her fans resumed conversing, albeit in slightly lowered tones. These were convivial people, more predisposed to gossip, discussion, witty asides, and opinionizing than silent appreciation. Not everyone displayed sparkling intellectual élan

or stiletto sharp wit, but most did, and even the dullest possessed an encyclopedic knowledge of pop culture and a
hipster's minimum of obscure facts about modern art and
political theory. One of the jewelry designers, for example,
was able to pick up the drug dealer, despite his boyfriend's
presence, by citing Hakim Bey on temporary autonomous
zones. Maxine somehow managed to observe this and—
while crooning Roxy Music's "Editions of You"—directed
the "boys will be boys will be boyoyoys" line right at the
lovebirds.

And though Maxine would have preferred everyone to
focus on her with rapt attention, she nevertheless put on a
stellar show. Like all the attendees, I felt singularly lucky to
be present at such a rarified performance. San Francisco
might be a small city and far from the beating heart of
contemporary culture, but just then and there, neither I
nor anyone present could even imagine wanting to be
somewhere else. Maxine might be an acquired taste with a
voice that didn't always do what it was supposed to, but she
was indisputably a superlative.

The show continued for a full hour before Maxine,
who'd absorbed enough psychic energy from her audience
to feel positively euphoric, did three encores before con-
cluding her set. After her finale, met with much applause,
she went to the women's room and locked the door. There
she dabbed her forehead with cold water, fixed her
makeup, and took a deep breath. The one thought on her
mind: *I have GOT to start playing venues with backstages so I
can decompress with dignity after a performance.*

Returning to the bar, she was accosted by Moon Pie whose eyes were wide with wonder. "You didn't tell me you were such a star! You're famous! And I just loved the show! You're so intellectual! I'm going to be living with a Big Deal!"

"Yeah, well . . ." said Maxine, doing her best to affect modesty.

"I gotta run to catch the bus back to Oakland, but I'll see you Wednesday. Bye honey!"

They air kissed and Moon Pie bolted off. Maxine commenced schmoozing. Though everyone was making a fuss over her, she still involuntarily missed Harris, just a tiny bit, for his delightful habit of vicariously basking in her success by endlessly discussing and sycophantically praising her performance.

An hour later, Maxine felt a grand headache coming on which was not improved when Hank, the bartender, called her aside and handed her three twenties. "Your share of the door."

She counted the bills then counted them again. "You've got to be joking. We had almost as many people as last month when I made one-sixty!"

"Don't put so many people on the guest list."

"Well could you at least round it up to a hundred?"

"You know, I'm running a business here. We had a deal."

The word "business" triggered Maxine's resentment toward the financially non-marginal. "You know, I'm sure you're making a mint with all the drinks *my fans* bought. And I very seriously doubt you could get anyone else to sing here for under three hundred dollars. Now I don't suppose you would even be aware, tucked away in this little bar, but I'm *a legend* in this town. I've played the Warfield! Still, I'm not even going to ask for another two-forty, which would be perfectly reasonable. I would, however, take it as an act of good faith if you offered me another hundred."

Hank groaned, then glanced down the bar. "Be right back." He went off to serve a customer.

Maxine glanced around the bar in desperation, only to see the last of her remaining friends dribbling out the door calling out good-byes and hurtling air kisses her way. Only the bar's regulars remained, a dozen alkies sporting faces deeply etched by toil and woe.

"You didn't charge them, did you?" Maxine asked Hank on his return. She pointed at the human wreckage.

"They're here every night," said Hank. "Every day too."

"So you didn't charge them. That's very unprofessional," said Maxine. "Very unprofessional indeed. I'm owed another forty . . . at least."

Hank opened the till and scowled down at the money. "Jeez!" He pulled out a two twenties and thrust them toward Maxine.

"Thanks," she said coldly. Normally she would've haggled for another half hour, but with the check in her purse she could, for once, afford to save her breath and dignity.

Andy appeared from nowhere. "Hi Maxi!"

"Here," said Maxine, handing him two twenties.

He took the money with a scowl. "You said I was guaranteed seventy-five."

"Showbiz," she said with a roll of his eyes.

"I hear ya," said Andy with a rueful grin. "But only forty?" Maxine handed him another twenty. "Hey thanks. I'd give you a ride home but I gotta pick up my girlfriend from the Century. She's waiting."

Maxine waived her hand. "Fine. Go. Go." He went.

Back at her apartment, Maxine felt relieved to find Harris was asleep, or at least pretending to be, on his sofa. For a second she wondered, *where would he go?* Then she reminded herself it was not her problem. He was a grown man and ought to be able to take care of himself. Anyway, she had enough to worry about, like how she was going to spend a *thousand dollars*!

CHAPTER 24

DISASTER

"I BROUGHT A LITTLE SOMETHING TO celebrate my moving in," announced Harris, holding up a bottle of whiskey. "I mean, I'm not really drinking these days, but sparkling water didn't seem up to the occasion."

"Hand it over," said Wally, grabbing the bottle and marching down the hall toward the kitchen. "We have to talk." Harris followed, hoping his friend's harsh tone didn't portend difficulties.

As Wally plopped some ice into the *Flintstone* jelly jars and poured the whiskey, Harris struck a lighthearted tone. "The jars again? What *are* we going to do with you? Well, never mind. As soon as I get settled, we'll find some decent serving glasses and totally redecorate. If I've said it once I've said it a thousand times, it's a crying shame how you've never fixed this place up. I'm not saying you're to blame. Obviously, you've tried to do something with all your movie posters and whatnot. But . . ."

Wally cut him off. "Listen, Harris, we have to talk about you moving in. It's not going to work."

Harris roared, *"What?"*

Wally's eyebrows knit in consternation. "Look, I never said you could move in *for sure*. I said I'd talk to my room-mates. I asked Casey and he said he didn't want you living here because you're a downer and Ted thinks you smoke too much and I would have gone and let you move in anyway *if you hadn't freaking ruined my show the other night!*" He started yelling. "What makes you think I'd even *consider* letting you move in after pulling a stunt like that?!"

"But I've already given Maxine notice," Harris shrieked. "I have to move out *now!*"

Wally steeled himself with a swig of whisky. "And what's with this *now* business? I had no idea we were talking about your moving in *right away*. I thought we were talking next month."

"This is an *emergency*," whined Harris.

Wally's face reddened with irritation and disgust. "And Lance told me you're planning to sue the theater, which would *totally* shut it down. Frankly, now that I think about it, I'm not sure I even want you in my house."

"Look, if that theater means so much to you, I'll drop the lawsuit."

Wally began shaking with rage. "Oh, so you were really going to go through with that? For real? Get out. Just get out."

Harris stood but didn't leave. "I would like to know exactly why I'm being forced into homelessness."

Wally's voice quivered as he slowly and deliberately delivered his final verdict. "You—are—a—scary—person."

Overcome by near-homicidal rage, Harris stood and began marching himself toward the front door. Wally followed with a glowering look on his face. With his hand on the doorknob, Harris made a dramatic turn and faced Wally. "And by the way . . . your play was *trash*. A sad orgy of feel-good nostalgia with *nothing* to say about the human condition, which is the whole *point* of theater."

This out-of-the-blue criticism took Wally by surprise, but in a flash he knew (much as he didn't want to!) that Harris's critique contained a smallish kernel of truth. As his mind began processing the implications, his expression changed from rageful to despondent. Harris, seeing that he'd scored a small victory, turned from his stricken friend and propelled himself out into the night.

CHAPTER 25

A DESPERATE PLEA

AT THE NEAREST CORNER MARKET, HARRIS purchased a can of beer to quell his rising panic. He then charged down the street until he found a payphone. Lance lived in a studio apartment, but it did have a little sofa. After a few fortifying sips of Heineken, he dialed.

"Butterfield home for wayward girls, Miss Butterfield speaking."

Though panicked, Harris tried *very hard* to sound casual. "Hey Lance, what's up?"

"Nothing. I'm just spending the night in bed reading."

Harris's honest reaction slipped out before he could stop it. "How utterly grim."

"It's not grim . . ." objected Lance, but Harris was already speaking over him.

"So I'm calling because, well, you know how Maxine is crazy? She ordered me to move out of our apartment by midnight on the 31st, which I'm pretty sure is not even legal. Without going into the sordid details, let me just say that, as you can imagine, I'm beside myself. Now, I know you have a couch . . ."

"No."

"It'd only be for a few days."

"No."

"But . . ."

"No."

"Look, I am facing *homelessness!*" Harris felt alarmed by the hysteria creeping into his own voice.

"Harris, no."

"I hope you're not thinking I'm going to be one of those people who move in for a short stay and then take forever to move out."

"That's exactly what I'm thinking. Maybe it's time to join the exodus. There's a whole world outside San Francisco and it's a lot cheaper out there. I've had three friends move to Oakland in the last year, and one to L.A. Oh, and another ran off to join the faeries in . . . I think it was Tennessee."

"I don't think you quite grasp my situation. Money is an issue."

"Look, we live in a greedy, stupid, and corrupt society. Nobody in power cares about affordable housing. I'm not even sure the plutocrats running this country even know there's a housing crisis. But I spend all day waiting tables for obnoxious yuppies. When I get home to my apartment—which as you know is barely bigger than a breadbox—I need my personal space. I suggest you find some way to patch things up with Maxine or . . . don't you have relatives somewhere? Florida? Maybe you need to pay them a visit."

Harris tried to interrupt, "Lance, Lance, Lance . . ."

Lance paid him no mind. "And I know they're awful, but there *are* residence hotels, though you should try getting one on Market Street, not in the Tenderloin. I know life in the Big City isn't easy, but you can't expect other people to save you, and you can't move in here. You just can't." The line went dead.

Harris stood frozen for a moment, groaned, finished his beer in one long swig then carefully considered other friends who might be willing to put him up. Nobody occurred to him except perhaps . . . Gunther. The very thought sent Harris into paroxysms of despair. *Oh my god,* he thought. *It's come to this. Gunther.*

Now, it is a sad fact of human nature that most people enjoy having some poor schnook to look down on, a loser so pathetic that their own flaws and foibles seem meager by comparison. For scores of scenesters, the schnook of choice was Harris. Amongst a certain set, no social gathering was complete until someone dragged out a funny Harris story. The contemplation of his self-serving dramatics affected people with a sort of pink champagne giddiness. Harris himself was forced to look far and wide before finding someone low enough to gaze down upon with malevolent condescension, but had finally discovered Gunther.

Freed from the necessity of earning his keep by a modest trust fund, Gunther began each day facing what some would consider a horizon of limitless possibility but which he preferred to see as an infinite void. He chose to fill that void (rather unoriginally, one must say) with cheap sex, expensive liquor, whatever drugs were at hand, and a thin veneer of Bohemian pretense. For over half a decade, Gunther had been, or at least claimed to have been, working on a trip-hop album. (Or rather it was originally to have been a trip-hop album but now that trip-hop was old news it had become "electronic, but beyond genre.") All Harris had heard from it were a few songs consisting of morose droning synthesizers played over beats so irregular and irritating they gave him heart palpitations. Nonetheless, Gunther's apartment contained a small, closet-less room he'd converted into a music studio. Perhaps, just perhaps, he could be persuaded to rent it out.

Harris instinctively felt that Gunther would be better approached in person than on the phone and set off for his flat just off Castro Street. Walking there Harris was forced to wend his way through endless clusters of happy homos bouncing between *chic* restaurants and pick-up bars, all yammering loudly and laughing Dolce Vita laughs, manifestly having the time of their lives. Their happiness was salt on his psychic wounds, and Harris was mightily relieved to finally arrive at his destination. He gave the doorbell three sharp rings and waited.

CHAPTER 25

THE DEPTHS OF DEPRAVITY

George, Gunther's dyspeptic roommate, opened the front door and wordlessly peered at him through thick spectacles.

"Is Gunther around?"

George scowled. "In his bedroom. And tell him to answer the door himself if he's expecting company. I'm not the butler." He retreated inside. Harris shut the front door and walked down the long hall to Gunther's bedroom door and knocked. "Guuuntherrr!"

The door creaked opened, revealing a psychotically squalid room. Dirty clothes, empty pizza boxes, porn magazines, DVDs, art supplies, sex toys, dirty dishes, and sundry knick-knacks were jumbled about chaotically. In the middle of this mess stood Gunther wearing a pair of black gym shorts, fancy tennis shoes, and an oversized lime green t-shirt emblazoned with the word "ENERGY" in sliver metallic lettering. His messy "bed head" hair, so blond as to look white, attractively framed his chiseled, Nordic features and icy blue eyes.

"Oh, it's you," said Gunther without enthusiasm. "Come on in."

I never let my room get this disorganized, thought Harris, feeling a sudden spark of pride. "You know," he said, "they say the state of your room reflects the state of your mind."

Gunther sat on the one chair. "I've been *trying* to clean up all day, but I had the worst trick in the world last night. I was feeling depressed so I dropped some ecstasy and went out to this tired club and the music was so horrible I couldn't even dance, so I was sitting at the bar and then this hunky guy sat down beside me and I asked him if he knew where I could get any steroids 'cause I've been getting fat lately which is totally unfair because I hardly even eat . . ."

"Alcohol has calories too, darling," interrupted Harris. For lack of a better option, he pushed a pile of soiled laundry off the bed and sat down, not without a hint of fear that he'd catch something from the sheets, which had certainly seen more than their share of dissipation.

"I don't drink that much," said Gunther defensively, a statement belied by a plethora of empty liquor bottles scattered amongst the refuse.

"Your room has an *odor*," noted Harris with a crinkle of his nose.

Gunther ignored him. "So anyway, even though this guy was built like a superhero he said he'd been a fat kid, so he was sympathetic and said he'd help. Plus, it turned out we take a lot of the same psych meds, so we had stuff in common. I invited him to come back here and fool

around, and he said yeah, but he had to say good-bye to
all his friends, and it turned out he'd come up from Palm
Springs with like, eight buddies and they were all over the
club so it took forever and I was like, can we go already?
And he kept saying he had to find one more buddy . . ."

As Gunther burbled on, Harris noticed a half-empty
bottle of Stoli on the floor between the bed and the nightstand. "Could I have a shot of voddy? I mean, I don't really
drink any more, but what with Maxine literally attacking
me and throwing me out onto the street I need something
to calm my nerves."

Gunther dug out a container of plastic champagne
glasses from a heap of detritus and tossed them to Harris
without breaking the flow of his narrative. "So we were
messing around and he says do you have any porn? And I
said what kind . . ."

As he poured himself a drink, Harris suppressed a
yawn. Gunther had been telling tales of his never-ending
quest for hotties for so many years they'd assumed the
comfortingly soporific quality of bedtime stories. After a
small eternity, the anecdote finally concluded with the
hunk spending several hours watching smutty videos while
ignoring Gunther and then taking off—possibly taking
Gunther's camera with him, though it was also possible it
was just misplaced.

"I haven't even slept yet," said Gunther in a petulant
tone, as if his inability to sleep while under the influence
of ecstasy was another injustice visited upon him by a
sadistic universe. "I *would have,* but my stupid-ass doctor

won't give me any downers. I told him it's my body and I know what I need, but he tells me to relax by taking a walk or reading a book. Just ridiculous."

"So get another doctor," said Harris, pouring himself more vodka.

"They're all the same," said Gunther. "Stingy with the drugs. They never prescribe enough so you'll have to keep coming back. It's all about making money."

I may be chronically depressed, but at least I'm not so crazy I have to go to a shrink, thought Harris. "So, as I alluded to earlier," he said in a deliberately casual tone, "Maxine went berserk and threw me out of our apartment."

Gunther remained placid. "What did you do to piss her off?"

"Nothing! She's a lunatic. You know that. She must have got a bad batch of hormones or something. So I was wondering if maybe, like just for a month, I could rent out your spare room." He'd only seen the room once or twice, but it had left a vivid impression because the luxury of one individual having two rooms struck him as fantastical.

"You mean my *music studio?*"

"It would only be for this one month, maybe even just a couple weeks, while I find a new place."

"I *need* that space. Besides, there's no bed in there."

"I'll bring a sleeping bag. And you can use the studio when I'm not there, which will be practically all the time because as you know I have a job and all the usual errands to run and an active social life and even if I'm there you can just ask me to go to the living room if the muse decides to pay you a visit even in the middle of the night which would be fine because, like you, I have a terrible time sleeping and will probably be awake anyway."

Gunther shook his head. "No way."

"Come on, this is an emergency," said Harris. "If I don't find someone to let me move in with them, I'll have to move into a *residency hotel.*"

"So?" said Gunther.

"So that's a fate worse than death!" said Harris. "At least let me stay here for a few days while I find somewhere else to go."

"George would never agree to it. We're not getting along."

"For a *few days?*" begged Harris.

"My brain is not ready to think about this right now," said Gunther, who tended to speak of his brain as if it were a colicky baby in need of pampering. Harris, sensing the futility of further discussion, compacted his seething rage into a disused corner of his mind. This was not giving up, merely a tactical retreat. He took out a cigarette and lit up.

"Lemme have one," said Gunther.

"When did you start smoking?"

"Last week. It's sexy. You get to stand outside bars and ask boys for a light."

Harris held out his pack. "But your lungs, think of your lungs! You should be treating your body like a temple, not a trash heap."

Gunther rolled his eyes as he took a cigarette. "Whatever."

"I've asked you time and again never to use that word in my presence," admonished Harris, his eyes taking on a steely cast and his voice a vaguely Teutonic bossiness. "You will refrain from doing so, please."

"Okay, okay. I won't say whatever."

Harris gave Gunther a light. "I saw *Dawn: Portrait of A Teenage Runaway.*"

"Why? Live theater is *so* tired."

"You're wrong there," said Harris, who'd taken a couple of drama classes in high school. "I adore Ibsen, Chekhov, Shaw . . . but this? This was *bad.*"

"Stupid phony air kissing theater queens," said Gunther, choking a little on the poisonous smoke. "I *hate* Wally." He smiled to let Harris know this was the start of their private game: Hate. It was Harris's turn.

"I *hate* how every time he sees you, he gives you a flyer for one of his pathetic shows."

Gunther volleyed. "I *hate* how Wally gets tipsy from like, *two* cocktails, but tells everyone he's a big lush."

Harris thought for a second. "I *hate* how they put obscene double entendres in every scene."

There was a knock on the door followed by George's strained voice. "Are you smoking in there? We agreed when we moved in that this was to be a non-smoking household."

"We agreed moving in that this was to be a non-smoking household," echoed Gunther in a mockingly prissy voice just loud enough for George to hear. Then, louder, "Look, you're in another room, you couldn't possibly be bothered by our smoke."

"I'm allergic," said George.

"Whatever," Gunther said.

"Do we have to put these out?" whispered Harris. "And I repeat: please don't use the word 'whatever' in my presence."

"Just hold 'em outside." Gunther opened a window facing the street. He and Harris sat on the floor smoking with their arms extended into the night.

"This is not gracious living," said Harris.

"Mean mommy can't have her precious, pure apartment defiled by cigarettes," spat Gunther bitterly.

"I don't know how you put up with him," said Harris. "Why not move him out and move me in?"

"He's on the lease or I would in a heartbeat."

Harris shook his head. "So you can't even smoke in your own room? I don't see how you can live under such tyranny. If I were you, I'd move. You and I could get a place together, a two bedroom."

"Are you crazy? Do you know how much two bedrooms are going for these days?"

"Like *you* need to worry about money."

"Uh . . . *yeah*," said Gunther. "I do. I get enough allowance so I don't have to work, but I'm still poor. If I had to live on any less than I do now I think I'd kill myself."

Harris couldn't believe his ears. "I live on less than half what you do, are you saying I should kill myself?"

"I can't say what's right for you, only what's right for me. I don't see the point of hanging on just for the sake of it. I'd kill myself if I were bald or fat or over forty or crippled . . ."

Harris poured himself a little more vodka. "You are so spiritually stunted. Though I have to give you points for being so upfront about being a trustafundian. Most rich kids are so secretive."

"I'm not ashamed. My ancestors *worked* for that money."

"Hmmm . . ." said Harris.

"Anyway," said Gunther, with a sly smile, "I plan to get a little cost of living increase." He pulled out two video-cassettes from a pile near his chair and held them aloft and waived them as if he were brandishing evidence before a jury. "Last time I visited my Dad I found *these* in my parents's closet."

"What on Earth were you doing in their closet?"

"It was Halloween and I was looking for a costume. I went as my mom."

"How very *Psycho*."

"Found these in a shoe box. Sex movies of my Dad getting into some really kinky shit."

Harris nearly choked. "I hope you didn't watch them!"

"Not all the way through. They're totally disgusting. This dominatrix-y woman, *not my mom*, hypnotizes him and makes him put on ladies lingerie. Forced feminization, they call it. The thing is, he's a child psychiatrist. All I have to do is tell him I'll send these to his clients unless he dissolves my trust and gives me my full inheritance *now*."

Harris felt a little better. *At least I've never sunk so low as to blackmail my own father.* "Frankly, I find the whole subject distasteful and I'd rather not hear about it."

"Okay," said Gunther. "Hey, you know what I hate? I *hate* Wally's pudgy little face."

"That was *so* not witty. You're not even trying. I *hate* how Wally told me I could move into his apartment and then backed out at the last second leaving me homeless."

Gunther sighed impatiently. "Am I going to have to hear about this all night?"

Harris whined, "Am I supposed to forget that I have *nowhere to live?*"

"It's not *my* problem."

Seething white-hot rage ignited in Harris's brain, incinerating all verbal thought. Instinctively, he charged out of the room. Gunther followed into the hall and watched as Harris slammed out the front door. George poked his head out of his room. "What's going on?" He saw the lit cigarette in Gunther's mouth and his face contorted as if hit with tear gas. "You're smoking!"

"Whatever," said Gunther, belligerently attempting to blow a smoke-ring. George retreated to his room, slamming his door in anger.

Gunther swore under his breath and returned to his own room, slamming his door in retaliation. Though feeling crash-y from drugs, he decided to hit a few bars before hitting the sack. He grabbed a jacket and headed out, slamming his door a second time just to irritate George, and locking it. The lock was unnecessary as George had no more interest in visiting his room than the ninth circle of hell, but Gunther enjoyed adding to the unfriendly atmosphere of the apartment. As he left, he slammed the front door of the apartment too, just for good measure.

Had Gunther not left his room in a huff, he might have noticed Harris's cigarette still balanced precariously on the sill of the open window, still merrily burning away. Only moments after Gunther departed, a small breeze rolled it two centimeters to the left. There, its lit end came in contact with the curtain. Within moments, tiny flames began licking their way along the edge of the old, dry fabric.

Now, there are neuroscientists and mystics who believe the human brain is far cannier than generally supposed. They assert that each of its eleven billion neurons is a super-intelligent computer capable of communicating with its cohorts through a virtually limitless combination of chemicals and electrical charges. Such a miraculous organ, they claim, is conscious of even the most insignificant thoughts, actions, and sensory impressions. If this be true (and I am far too ignorant to hazard a guess one way or another) it would mean that anyone who left a burning cigarette on a windowsill would be aware, subconsciously, they were performing a small act of domestic terrorism.

George, having lit incense in order to mask the seeping stink of cigarette smoke, did not immediately notice the acrid burning smell emanating from Gunther's room. When he finally detected the malodorous scent wafting into his nostrils, he steeled himself for unpleasantness and knocked on his roommate's door. There was no response.

Through the magic of literature, let us now see both sides of the door simultaneously. Poor bespectacled, beleaguered George on one side, his nose wrinkled in disgust. On the other, yellowish orange flames spread from the drapes to the bed sheets. George, starting to suspect the worst, calls Gunther's name. Flames devour the pillows. Losing patience, George tries the door only to discover it's locked. Flames start in on the wall posters. George throws himself against the door, which remains locked shut. Clothes, magazines, and pizza boxes near Gunther's bed ignite. George whips out his cellphone and dials 911 in a panic.

I will spare my readers the hackneyed spectacle of blackened smoke billowing forth from the windows and brave firemen rushing in to evacuate traumatized apartment dwellers. Instead, we will follow Harris, oblivious to everything but his own anger, tromping back to Maxine's apartment. On arriving, he discovered to his great relief that she was out (spending the evening at the Black Rose, in case you're wondering). For several hours he lay on his sofa smoking cigarette after cigarette as a psychic tempest raged in his mind. He had nowhere to live. His friends and family had abandoned him. The world was an evil, wicked place and there was no hope. As bleak thoughts ricocheted around his mind, Harris fell into a slumber plagued by toxic nightmares. *No hope, no hope, no hope.*

CHAPTER 26

HARRIS IN FLIGHT

THE FIRST OF SEPTEMBER, HARRIS AWOKE unusually early. After ascertaining that Maxine was either still asleep or not at home (thank heavens!) he gritted his teeth and phoned a series of low-end residency hotels until he found one on Market Street with a vacancy. There were no boxes handy, so he stuffed his meager belongings into shopping bags, which made them look even more meager. While retrieving his toiletries in the bathroom, he inadvertently caught sight himself in the mirror of the medicine cabinet over the sink. Dark bags gave his eyes a raccoon-ish look while his face (hadn't it been taut and young just the other day?) was visibly sagging and his skin had turned the pale gray of cigarette ash. An aura of decay and despoliation radiated from his person. *You look some washed up alkie chainsmoking in a Greyhound bus depot at four in the morning,* he thought.

Harris lugged his belongings down to the street and taxied to the hotel. *Nothing more than a fleabag,* Harris thought as he walked through the door, his dread now

185

compounded by a deep sense of shame. What if someone he knew were to see him entering such a disreputable building? Stepping into the tiny lobby, Harris recoiled. The place reeked of mildew and curry and the low ceiling made him claustrophobic. He went up to the plexiglass window of the front office and secured a room from an indifferent middle-aged clerk. He was just able to swing the two-week's move-in cost but would now be paying considerably more on a monthly basis than he had at Maxine's.

He rode the elevator to the third floor and emerged into a hallway lit by an uncovered light bulb utterly incapable of dispelling the decades of accumulated gloom. Unhappy ghosts lurked in the corners and, more disturbingly, a neighbor scuttling toward the communal bathrooms moved with such jerkiness Harris was forced to conclude he either suffered from a rare neurological disorder or (more likely) a crack addiction. With mounting horror, Harris located his room, unlocked the door, and switched on the overhead light. The space was, if not horrific, dispiritingly charmless. The bed, nightstand, dresser, and floor lamp were modern but cheap, the walls a sickly pale yellowish green, the industrial carpeting entirely colorless, and the single window looked out onto an airshaft.

There was a small closet (that didn't even have a door!) in which Harris quickly hung his more wrinkle-able items. *This is only temporary,* he assured himself. He then arranged his toiletries on top of the dresser and put his foldables in the drawers. *This is only temporary.* Lastly, he left his decorative bric-a-brac in the bag (there was no room to put it anywhere) but taped his gallery of Inspiring People to the wall by his bed. The room still looked sub-pathetic. *This is only temporary.* He sat down on the mattress and immediately discerned it was so thin he could feel the springs within. He would never sleep again. For the first time since childhood, Harris found himself actually crying. Before his sobs could subside, he left the hotel and went down to use a phone booth in the Civic Center BART station.

"Mother? It's me . . . How perceptive of you to notice. No, things are *not* going well. Things are about as bad as things can get. I wouldn't hesitate to call what's happened a disaster of the first magnitude . . . Yes, we *do* have to discuss this *right this very instant* . . . Well, in a nutshell, I've had to move rather suddenly. Maxine went berserk and I literally had to flee for my life . . . No, I wasn't on the lease . . . No, the police don't care. Nobody cares. They let the crazies run loose in this hideous town . . . Yes, *hideous.* I told you before, the city you saw when you visited is not the *real* San Francisco, not the city I live in on daily basis . . . I'm *not* exaggerating. There are junkies panhandling outside the door! . . . Yes, within thirty feet of the door . . . Well yes, exactly, I need to move! Right away! Unfortunately, that would require money . . . I'm not sure, but enough for first and last month's rent and a security deposit . . . I'd pay you back. No, I *can't* stay here till the fifteenth. *This is not a nice hotel!* . . . Hello, am I not speaking English? I, *your son,* am sitting on the bed of a scary *welfare hotel.* My life is *literally in danger* . . . Well, that's a fine thing to say . . . It's not like I was given a great start in life. I won't even mention my genetic heritage . . . For one thing I'm short, but look, we're getting off subject here . . . I *would* be able to pay you back . . . If I had a nice place to stay, I could sleep better and then I *could* work full time and make enough money to pay rent and even save because I'd get a credit card . . . Yes, credit cards *do save you money* because you can buy things *on sale.* I don't know how many times I've come across a pair of shoes I liked that I couldn't buy because I didn't have the cash on me and when I went back, they were gone, and I ended up buying something *even more* expensive. Mother? Mother? Are you there?" Harris hung up the phone and whispered to himself, "I am an orphan."

Harris returned to his hotel room and sat forlornly on his torturously substandard bed. Suddenly, the sound of an idiotic TV game show began blaring through the wall. He didn't need to leave for McWhitty yet, but he decided to go for a stroll just to escape the torturous dungeon of a room. Fortuitously, he remembered someone mentioning that Oliver was having a book release party at A Different Light. Perfect! He could go poke around the store and hang out with the literary crowd (as people of quality did!) but could escape before the no-doubt-tedious reading of the book began with the perfectly valid excuse of needing to get to work.

CHAPTER 27

THE SHOCKING CONCLUSION

SERIOUS LITERATURE, SERIOUS MINDS AGREE, REQUIRES a steady, unblinking gaze at life's dark side. Greed, fear, megalomania, stupidity, despair, bloodlust, and loneliness pour from the pages of Homer, Tolstoy, and current best-sellers alike. Oliver (like yours truly) wrote to cheer himself up, and thus preferred to focus on less cataclysmic human frailties like pretension, laziness, and narcissism, and even these he generally wrapped in a candy coating of clever wordplay. Thus, serious publishers tended to dismiss him as fluff. Publishers of fluff, however, tended to find him overly esoteric as he wrote about gay hipsters and weirdoes, a niche market even smaller than gay Republicans or Bears. Scores of carefully-phrased queries to literary agents, small presses, and journals won Oliver nothing more than a thick wad of tersely-worded rejection letters. After a few years of this, most people would have stopped writing and turned their attentions to something offering more immediate rewards and a better chance of success, raising bonsai trees, say, or online blackjack. Oliver, though, was not most people. Rather than sink into a slough of despondence and bitterness, he constructed a cotton candy castle of delusion and crowned himself princess. He would be a literary lioness whether the world cared to notice or not.

Then, miraculously, Silent Scream, an up-and-coming "micro-publisher," agreed to put out *Dougie Doodles*. There would be but a thousand copies printed and there was no money for advertising, promotion, a book tour, or even an advance, and yet Oliver was elated that at least his work would be available in stores, and he could at long last join the immortal ranks of *published* authors. The word danced seductively in his mind, *published, published, published,* conjuring a fantasy scene in which he stood around cocktail parties with literati and glitterati discussing movie rights and the best way to handle groupies. Intoxicating!

Oliver was not sure about the cover, though. The publisher, hoping for *sexy,* had chosen a handsome, slender, shirtless youth staring at a starry night sky in which the moon had been replaced by a mirrored disco ball. Yet all doubts vanished when Oliver saw a copy prominently displayed in the window of A Different Light on mega-super-ultra-gay Castro Street. *I have arrived,* he thought to himself, with as much relief as pride.

On the night of his release party, Oliver, using a cane rather than his usual wheelchair, tottered into the bookstore wearing an electric blue mini-dress, pink feathered boa, three-inch cha-cha heels, and a short, chunky blond wig worn backwards so that it looked more '60s. "You look marvelous," trilled Vivian, putting down the lesbian detective novel she'd been killing time with.

Oliver preened. "I'm ready for my close-up, Mrs. De Mille."

The superhumanly handsome salesclerk (no other kind were allowed on Castro Street) leaned over the counter. "You must be Oliver! Thanks for coming. We've already sold like three copies, which is pretty good for a small press thing."

"Stupendous," said Oliver. He peered at the back of the store where a dozen of his friends sat in folding chairs. "And thank you for letting me read here. Perhaps we could have sex later so I could show my appreciation."

"You're funny," said the clerk without cracking a smile. "Oh, someone named Adam Martinek called to say he was stuck in traffic but . . ." As the lad spoke, a short man in a rumpled suit burst into the store holding a platter of cheese, crackers, and cookies.

"But that I would be arriving soon," finished Adam. "Look, I brought hors d'oeuvres!"

"This is my publisher," said Oliver. Hellos were said while Adam looked around helplessly for somewhere to set his platter.

"I'll fetch a table for that," said the clerk, darting into a storage room.

"This is so exciting," said Vivian, snapping a photo of Oliver.

"Go sit," said Oliver, "It's tiresome of you to stand there worshipping me, even if I have just written a masterpiece."

"Okay, Sugar," said Vivian. She joined the crowd in the back of the store.

The clerk returned with a tiny folding table on which Adam set his tray. "I'm going back to the car for the rest of the goodies," he announced. "This is gonna be faboo!"

As he watched his fans set upon the food like sharks on chum, Oliver noticed that he wasn't breathing. *Could I be nervous?* he wondered, *Just because this is my first bookstore reading of my first book? How absurd.* He closed his eyes and began deeply and deliberately inhaling and exhaling while imagining pink cosmic energy from the stars beaming into his body. *I will be magnificent. I will be magnificent. I'd better be magnificent. Will I be magnificent?* The pink energy wasn't working very well.

"Hey," said Harris, startling Oliver. "Congratulations."

"Thank you," said Oliver, slowly and reluctantly lifting his eyelids. "So good of you to come."

"Unfortunately, I can't stay," said Harris, "I'm late for work already. But you know I read your book and I wanted to say I think it's terrific you finally finished it. So many people talk about writing books but never follow through."

Oliver beamed. "Would you like me to sign your copy?"

"I didn't actually buy one," said Harris. "But they let you read in the store here, not like some other places I could mention."

"You read the whole thing?" asked Oliver, noting that Harris's face wore a plastered-on smile and shifty eyes.

"Well, I skimmed through parts," said Harris. "I mean, there were some stories where not much seemed to happen.

A lot of the characters just going here and doing that. I skipped those." Oliver experienced the curious sensation of his body deflating like a rubber blow-up doll with a leak. "And I guess I had a hard time reading it straight through because a lot of the prose was so, I dunno, simple. Have you ever read Nabokov? Now *that's* prose! You should try reading Nabokov. Or were you going for a young adult audience? It did kind of read like a Hardy Boys or Nancy Drew novel." He paused, but Oliver had been rendered speechless. "And hey, what is up with that cover? What were you *thinking*?"

Oliver managed to choke out, "The publisher chose the cover."

Harris was indignant. "Correct me if I'm wrong, but it's your book. You should get to choose the cover."

"It doesn't work that way. Usually the publisher decides."

"Well, did you have to go with such a cheesy publisher?" asked Harris with a wry little grin. "You're a smart person, couldn't you have gotten Simon & Schuster or Random House?"

"No," said Oliver. "I don't have an agent and . . ." He stalled, not wanting to expound upon his lowly place in the literary universe.

"What you should've done," said Harris, "Was publish a few stories in magazines first. You know, *The New Yorker* . . ."

Oliver stammered. "Harris, your grasp on reality is . . ."

"At least I hope they paid you a bundle," said Harris.

Oliver's voice faltered. "One doesn't always make much on a first book."

"Well, I'm sure you at least got five-thousand dollars," interrupted Harris. He peered at the Oliver's stricken face. "No? Doll, you blew it! You wuz robbed! You're being *exploited.*"

Oliver glanced over at his small audience and tried using his eyes to implore someone to come to his rescue. Alas, everyone was occupied with chatting and/or hors d'oeuvres.

Harris went on. "And there was that one story, Dougie Doodles or something like that? I didn't get that one at all. I mean, maybe it was supposed to be funny? I love humor writing, though I do think it's more effective when it's not so joke-y, if you catch my drift. Have you heard of David Sedaris? You should really read David Sedaris. Now *he's* funny."

Time stood still for Oliver and an eerie silence blanketed the world, muffling Harris, his friends' voices, and the outside traffic. The edges of his vision blurred and dimmed so that all that he could see was Harris's face, his smug, smug little face. And then Oliver, who had never in his life struck another human, made a quick decision to visit justice upon Harris. Perhaps decision is not the right word, for Oliver's assault was more instinctual than deliberated. In any case, his enfeebled fists began flailing against Harris with what little strength he could muster. "Shut up, shut up, shut up!"

Harris, too shocked to defend himself or even turn away, stood frozen, his eyes mad with bewilderment. This warrants explanation: on first moving to town, Harris's droll humor and spirited bonhomie won him many pals. His transformation into embittered harpy was gradual enough that his less perceptive friends barely noticed and even the more astute weren't unduly alarmed. Urban denizens are largely too preoccupied with the bustle of everyday life to evaluate their compatriots' characters at regular intervals. Also, his nastiness was camouflaged by the mock-bitchery that passed for wit within his social set, his malice laughed off as a comedic pose. And so, with the de facto consent of his peers, he'd spent two decades misbehaving with impunity. Thus, his surprise at Oliver's assault may readily be imagined.

Harris's shock lasted but a few seconds. Words came to quell the panic with context and began flowing out of his mouth. "Help! Save me! I'm a victim!" He backed up against a wall of books using his arms to block Oliver's feeble fists.

"Vicious!"

"Lay off! Help! Stop!"

"Rotten!"

"You're insane! Stop!"

"Monster!"

"Help!"

"*Demon!*"

(This last epithet may sound extreme, but consider this: there is, according to reputable demonologists, a Grand Duke of Hell by the name of Haborym. Practitioners of the Dark Arts invoke him for his ability to "maketh men witty, set great castles and cities afire, and answer truly of private matters." This viper-riding, three-headed fire demon is also said to command twenty-six legions of sub-demons. One would have to be a devout atheist indeed to completely rule out the possibility that Harris could be one of Haborym's minions sent Earthward to bedevil humanity.)

On hearing the commotion, everyone in the store turned and began peeking around bookcases and standing tippy toe to see what was happening. Despite the appalling nature of the event, no one who'd come to hear Oliver read tried to stop the fracas. Hip San Franciscans are relentlessly pacifistic and regard intervention of any kind as a breach of good taste. Who am I to judge? They ask in any and every circumstance. Also true, those present who were acquainted with Harris knew how vexing he could be and sort of sympathized with Oliver . . . though only Maxine was so lacking in gentility as to break out laughing and scream, "Go Oliver! Womp that sucker! Git 'im!"

The handsome salesclerk, however, knew his duty and rushed out from behind the counter. "Cut it out!" he cried while making wild and ineffectual hand motions. Oliver ignored him. A split-second later Adam re-entered the store with another tray of canapés. He stood dumbstruck for a moment, then set his tray down on a table of remainders and pulled Oliver away from Harris. After a second of shocked silence, everyone began discussing the fight in urgent whispers.

Adam walked Oliver, red-faced and panting, out to the store's back patio. There he spoke in soothing tones until

Oliver regained his usual mask of existential aloofness. They decided that despite this unfortunate incident, the show must go on. "This could even be legendary," mused Oliver. "Did anyone get photos?"

Meanwhile Harris, stood stock still, utterly paralyzed with mortification "Am I bleeding?" he finally managed to ask.

"You're fine," assured the clerk, eager to minimize the shameful incident. "Come on. Let's get you some water." He took Harris by the arm and led him into a tiny bathroom. "What happened out there?" asked the clerk as he watched Harris splash his face in the sink and search for visible bruises (of which there were none) in the mirror.

"Oliver just attacked me for *no reason*," said Harris. "Has anyone called the police?"

"No reason?"

"I guess he must have dementia."

The door opened and Vivian came in. "You all right, Sugar?"

Harris laughed bitterly. "Sure. What could be wrong? I've just been *physically assaulted* in the middle of a bookstore. Happens all the time, right?"

"I'd better get back," said the clerk slipping out the door. "Take care!"

"Did you tell Oliver his book reminded you of a Hardy Boys mystery?" asked Vivian.

"Whatever I may or may not have said, and to be perfectly frank I don't even recall at this point I'm so upset, hardly matters in the face of *someone viciously attacking me and beating me with their fists.* This has got to be the most degrading and insane situation I've ever encountered. Are the police on their way?"

"I don't know, sweetie. But maybe you'd better just go."

"Well, I certainly hope they're not going to let that *person* read now. He's clearly a menace. He should be locked up for his own good and the good of the public."

The clerk popped his head through the door and stage whispered, "Oliver's about to start!" and popped out.

"Come on," said Vivian. She took Harris by the arm and pulled him out of the bathroom and through the store. Though mortified at having been part of a vulgar scene and keeping his head down, Harris couldn't help stealing a peek at the crowd. People were staring at him with curiosity, disdain, and amusement. This was going to make the best Harris story *ever.* A few agonizing seconds later, he and Vivian were out on the sidewalk. Vivian smiled soothingly and put her hand on Harris's arm. "I'm going back inside. But you take care of yourself, okay?"

Harris sputtered. *"I'm being thrown out* and the person who attacked me gets *honored with a reading?* This is a travesty!"

"Bye, sweetie." Vivian slipped back inside.

The sound applause came from inside the store, after which Oliver began speaking. Harris couldn't make out the words, but when the audience erupted in raucous laughter he just *knew* they were laughing at him. A hot flush of shame ran through his entire body and he decided to forgo calling the police. Oliver would get his later. He turned and faced the street, bustling with life in spite of the slowly descending shroud of cold fog. There was nothing to do but seek out a consoling cocktail. He started on his way, thinking, *I must get away/these people are monsters/This is the worst day of my life/I'm such a loser/ I hate everyone.*

AFTERWORD

I WOULD BE REMISS IN MY duty as narrator were I to end this book without a warning. Benighted souls like Harris are not as rare as one might hope. They tend to congregate in places devoted to mirth and merriment but are prone to drift and can be found almost anywhere. We are all destined to encounter a few Harrises on life's highway. Such creatures are ravenous for company and you may be tempted to befriend one, for they can be most amusing, but do so *at your own peril*. At first the Harris will seem harmless, perhaps even charming. This will not last. Your Harris, like all Harrises, wants desperately to pull you down into whatever dark, fetid Hell he has fashioned for himself that you might share his ceaseless torments and afflictions. Resisting would be easy except that (horrible truth!) we all have a little Harris inside us yearning for just such a fate. No, kind and gentle reader, when you encounter a Harris, you must smile politely and be on your way, else you will soon learn what it is to dwell amongst the damned.

THE END

ACKNOWLEDGEMENTS

I'D LIKE TO THANK: PETER CARLAFTES and Ashlyn Petro for their eagle-eyed editing, Kat Georges for her gorgeous cover design, my writing buddies from The Leporine Conspiracy, Dodie Bellamy's writing workshop, and the San Francisco State creative writing department for all their brilliant comments and critiques; my brother Bo, for keeping my computer running; the folks at Litquake, for including me in the festivities; and last-but-not-least, Tony Vaguely, without whose moral support and affection I would simply collapse.

ABOUT THE AUTHOR

ALVIN ORLOFF BEGAN WRITING IN 1977, while still a teenager, by penning lyrics for The Blowdryers, an early San Francisco punk band. He spent the 1980s working as a telemarketer and exotic dancer while concurrently attending U.C. Berkeley and performing with The Popstitutes, a somewhat absurd performance art/homocore band. In 1990 he and his bandmates founded Klubstitute, a floating queer cabaret devoted to the ideal of cultural democracy that featured spoken word, theater, drag, and musical acts. Orloff is the author of three previous novels, *I Married an Earthling, Gutter Boys*, and *Why Aren't You Smiling?* in addition to *Disasterama! Adventures in the Queer Underground 1977–1997*, a LAMBDA Literary Prize Finalist for Best Memoir. Orloff currently lives in San Francisco and works in the heart of the historic Castro District as the proprietor of Fabulosa Books.

RECENT AND FORTHCOMING BOOKS FROM THREE ROOMS PRESS

FICTION

Lucy Jane Bledsoe
No Stopping Us Now

Rishab Borah
The Door to Inferna

Meagan Brothers
Weird Girl and What's His Name

Christopher Chambers
Scavenger
Standalone

Ebele Chizea
Aquarian Dawn

Ron Dakron
Hello Devilfish!

Robert Duncan
Loudmouth

Michael T. Fournier
Hidden Wheel
Swing State

Aaron Hamburger
Nirvana Is Here

William Least Heat-Moon
Celestial Mechanics

Aimee Herman
Everything Grows

Kelly Ann Jacobson
Tink and Wendy
Robin and Her Misfits

Jethro K. Lieberman
Everything Is Jake

Eamon Loingsigh
Light of the Diddicoy
Exile on Bridge Street

John Marshall
The Greenfather

Alvin Orloff
Vulgarian Rhapsody

Micki Ravizee
Of Blood and Lightning

Aram Saroyan
Still Night in L.A.

Robert Silverberg
The Face of the Waters

Stephen Spotte
Animal Wrongs

Richard Vetere
The Writers Afterlife
Champagne and Cocaine

Jessamyn Violet
Secret Rules to Being a Rockstar

Julia Watts
Quiver
Needlework
Lovesick Blossoms

Gina Yates
Narcissus Nobody

MEMOIR & BIOGRAPHY

Nassrine Azimi and Michel Wasserman
Last Boat to Yokohama: The Life and Legacy of Beate Sirota Gordon

William S. Burroughs & Allen Ginsberg
*Don't Hide the Madness:
William S. Burroughs in Conversation with Allen Ginsberg*
edited by Steven Taylor

James Carr
BAD: The Autobiography of James Carr

Judy Gumbo
Yippie Girl: Exploits in Protest and Defeating the FBI

Judith Malina
Full Moon Stages: Personal Notes from 50 Years of The Living Theatre

Phil Marcade
Punk Avenue: Inside the New York City Underground, 1972–1982

Jillian Marshall
Japanthem: Counter-Cultural Experiences; Cross-Cultural Remixes

Alvin Orloff
Disasterama! Adventures in the Queer Underground 1977–1997

Nicca Ray
Ray by Ray: A Daughter's Take on the Legend of Nicholas Ray

Stephen Spotte
*My Watery Self:
Memoirs of a Marine Scientist*

PHOTOGRAPHY-MEMOIR

Mike Watt
On & Off Bass

SHORT STORY ANTHOLOGIES

SINGLE AUTHOR

Alien Archives: Stories
by Robert Silverberg

First-Person Singularities: Stories
by Robert Silverberg
with an introduction by John Scalzi

Tales from the Eternal Café: Stories
by Janet Hamill, with an introduction
by Patti Smith

*Time and Time Again:
Sixteen Trips in Time*
by Robert Silverberg

*The Unvarnished Gary Phillips:
A Mondo Pulp Collection*
by Gary Phillips

*Voyagers:
Twelve Journeys in Space and Time*
by Robert Silverberg

MULTI-AUTHOR

*Crime + Music: Twenty Stories
of Music-Themed Noir*
edited by Jim Fusilli

Dark City Lights: New York Stories
edited by Lawrence Block

*The Faking of the President: Twenty
Stories of White House Noir*
edited by Peter Carlaftes

*Florida Happens:
Bouchercon 2018 Anthology*
edited by Greg Herren

*Have a NYC I, II & III:
New York Short Stories;*
edited by Peter Carlaftes
& Kat Georges

*No Body, No Crime: Twenty-two Tales
of Taylor Swift-Inspired Noir*
edited by Alex Segura & Joe Clifford

*Songs of My Selfie:
An Anthology of Millennial Stories*
edited by Constance Renfrow

*The Obama Inheritance:
15 Stories of Conspiracy Noir*
edited by Gary Phillips

*This Way to the End Times:
Classic and New Stories of
the Apocalypse*
edited by Robert Silverberg

MIXED MEDIA

John S. Paul
*Sign Language: A Painter's Notebook
(photography, poetry and prose)*

DADA

*Maintenant: A Journal of
Contemporary Dada Writing & Art
(annual, since 2008)*

HUMOR

Peter Carlaftes
A Year on Facebook

FILM & PLAYS

Israel Horovitz
*My Old Lady: Complete Stage Play and
Screenplay with an Essay on Adaptation*

Peter Carlaftes
Triumph For Rent (3 Plays)
Teatrophy (3 More Plays)

Kat Georges
*Three Somebodies: Plays about Notorious
Dissidents*

TRANSLATIONS

Thomas Bernhard
On Earth and in Hell
(poems of Thomas Bernhard
with English translations by
Peter Waugh)

Patrizia Gattaceca
Isula d'Anima / Soul Island

César Vallejo | Gerard Malanga
Malanga Chasing Vallejo
(selected poems of César Vallejo
with English translations
and additional notes by
Gerard Malanga)

George Wallace
EOS: Abductor of Men
(selected poems in Greek & English)

ESSAYS

Richard Katrovas
*Raising Girls in Bohemia:
Meditations of an American Father*

Far Away From Close to Home
Vanessa Baden Kelly

*Womentality: Thirteen Empowering Stories
by Everyday Women Who Said Goodbye to
the Workplace and Hello to Their Lives*
edited by Erin Wildermuth

POETRY COLLECTIONS

Hala Alyan
Atrium

Peter Carlaftes
DrunkYard Dog
I Fold with the Hand I Was Dealt
Life in the Past Lane

Thomas Fucaloro
It Starts from the Belly and Blooms

Kat Georges
Our Lady of the Hunger
Awe and Other Words Like Wow

Robert Gibbons
Close to the Tree

Israel Horovitz
Heaven and Other Poems

David Lawton
Sharp Blue Stream

Jane LeCroy
Signature Play

Philip Meersman
This Is Belgian Chocolate

Jane Ormerod
Recreational Vehicles on Fire
Welcome to the Museum of Cattle

Lisa Panepinto
On This Borrowed Bike

George Wallace
Poppin' Johnny

Three Rooms Press | New York, NY | Current Catalog: www.threeroomspress.com
Three Rooms Press books are distributed by Publishers Group West: www.pgw.com